INCIDENT AT BROWNSFIELD ACADEMY

A Novel by
eddie knapps
© Copyright 2006

INCIDENT AT BROWNSFIELD ACADEMY

FIRST EDITION

A Boner Book by
The Nazca Plains Corporation
Las Vegas, Nevada
2006

ISBN:1-887895-60-4

Published by,

The Nazca Plains Corporation ®
4640 Paradise Rd, Suite 141
Las Vegas, NV 89169-8000

PUBLISHER'S NOTE
INCIDENT AT BROWNSFIELD ACADEMY is a work of fic-tion created wholly by the author's imagination. All characters are fictional and any resemblance to any persons living or deceased is purely by accident. No portion of this book reflects any real person or events.

Cover Photo by Corwin
Cover model Andy
Art Direction, Blake Stevens

DEDICATION

For Steve and Larry, who took a very green kid in hand and showed him what red was all about.

ACKNOWLEDGEMENTS

Thanks to all of those who have, over the years, shared in the worlds of fetish, discipline, and mansex. Specials nods are due to Rick, Frank, Tom, Don, David, Al, Mark, Bob, Andy, Wil, Mr. B, Uncle Matt, the late Colin Burns, and a host of other MEN WHO SPANK! too numerous to mention. It is a realm of great guys—thoughtful, honest, loyal—who are also hot, sexy, kinky, and have minds almost as dirty as my own. To all of you, my hat is off… and my pants are down.

Table of Contents

INCIDENT AT BROWNSFIELD ACADEMY

FIRST EDITION

A Novel by
eddie knapps

A Boner Book

THE INCIDENT

Ned Belknaps thought that the most humiliating moment of his life was that instant when Mr. Knighten, the Commandant of Brownsfield Academy, pulled open the toilet stall door and caught him--cock in hand, two fingers diddling his butthole--around 1:00p. m. on a Tuesday afternoon.

Little did Ned know, at that point, he had no NOTION of the meaning of the word HUMILIATION!

He had only been teaching at Brownsfield Academy for six weeks. He was a mid-semester replacement for some old-fart Navy guy who had had a heart attack. Brownsfield was certainly not his first choice for a job, but, since he was new to the area, it was what was available. At thirty-five, recently divorced, he was setting out on a new life, and if Brownsfield Academy needed a history teacher, it would do until he found something he preferred.

Brownsfield itself, founded at the end of the Nineteenth Century, prided itself as a "conservative, traditional institution," as its advertisements said, that emphasized "old-fashioned virtues of academic excellence, athletic prowess, and self-control, duty and discipline." With both boarders and day students, it maintained a proud legacy of providing military officers to all branches of the service, and its smartly turned out cadet corps was well-known about town both for its high spirits and for its strength and stamina on any one of a number of levels!

Ned had taken a break from his history class to find a little relief in the faculty men's room. Standing every day in front of those bright-faced young men in their military uniforms, he had discovered their hard, developed bodies and hearing them say "Yes, Sir" and "No, Sir" to him gave him a real sense of authority, and, somewhat confusingly for him, a NOTABLE itch in the crotch. The power and respect he enjoyed was almost like a drug! It was certainly different from his experience teaching in the public schools! At least there was, for stodgy old Brownsfield (which he frankly held in ill-disguised contempt), SOMETHING to be said.

From time to time, it was almost embarrassing as his six and a half inch penis grew within his pants. Aside from a little "messing around" early in puberty, Ned had never really considered male to male sex. He had begun fucking girls in high school, and had always thought he got as much enjoyment from it as most. Still, he had to admit, one of the reasons his five year marriage had fallen apart was that his "in bed" life with his wife had very soon lost its magic. He had had a couple of affairs, but nothing particularly serious, and, at this point, was largely dependent on his hand and a racy video now and then to relieve the tension in his balls.

Belknaps was sure some of the boys in his classes had noticed his excitement and discomfort as he tried to shift his obvious erection in his trousers. Two of the seniors in particular, Toby Steele and Mike Green in his fifth period class, seemed always to have their eyes on his crotch when he got a hard-on. Perhaps they had said something to Mr. Knighten, officially known as "The Commandant," and that was how he happened to surprise Mr. Belknaps that day.

There in the bathroom, for just a second, nothing was said, as Mr. Knighten, a look of fury on his face, surveyed the thirty-five year old teacher seated there on the toilet. There was certainly no question, in this battle-hardened warrior's mind, as to what was going on. Belknaps' penis was hard as a rock, and there was no denying—Jesus Christ!--he was stimulating himself up the ass as well. What kind of pervert had he hired!

Ned's fingers exited the door of his hole with a slight plop as he looked in horror at his superior, framed in the doorway.

"GODDAMN IT!" Knighten exploded. "I don't put up with this kind of shit from the cadets, and I'm SURE not going to put up with it from my faculty!"

Knighten was a large man--a couple of inches over six feet tall with broad shoulders and, these days, something of a belly, weighing in at 230 pounds. Everything about him was BIG: his face heavy-browed and large-jawed, his arms still well-muscled and brawny, his legs thick and powerful. He was, without question, a BEAR of a man in almost every way, with thick, dark hair pelting his chest and stomach, his arms and legs, even sprinkled on his shoulders and trailing down his back, gruff in his manner and simply exuding a powerful, no-nonsense masculinity. Beyond that, more than twenty years in the Marine Corps had trained him in the virtues of discipline and self-control. And, for Knighten, you could gauge a man's self-control by how he dealt with his penis.

During his life, his own manhood had only known the stimulation of a woman's pussy. Though a lifelong bachelor, his meaty 7 inches, thick and veiny, had pounded many a twat over the years. These were far from the only orgasms he had experienced, particularly in the last few years, but, with these, they occurred SPONTANEOUSY, with ABSOLUTELY no encouragement from his OWN palm or fingers. The Commandant lived by a simple rule: MANUAL MANIPULATION of the MALE MEMBER was ABOMINABLE! This was a lesson he had learned early on from a VERY strict father who had, upon encountering him with his pants down in the basement playing with his pecker, taught him a lesson he had NEVER forgotten in all the years since! After his dad was done with him, standing, weeping, his bare bottom ABLAZE from slash after slash of a willow switch, Knighten was told in no uncertain terms a male must NEVER play with his penis for his own pleasure. Seed should be spilled ONLY as a result of efforts of others.

This was a code he had lived by ever since.

Hence, ANY cadet "caught in the act" knew what awaited him in the Commandant's office, whether he had ever been punished for it or not. The CRACKS and CRIES echoing down the hallways of Brownsfield Academy would leave no doubt in anyone's mind about that, let alone the tearstained faces that exited that door when the discipline was done. Knighten ran Brownsfield with an iron hand, and, as far as he was concerned, not only his young cadets but his teachers--all men--were sub-ject to the rules of the academy. He had had deep suspicions that this recent hire might be a problem--sarcastic, disrespectful of tradition, skating close to being insubordinate. In sum, a real smart-aleck.

And now THIS!

The Commandant had no intention of letting Belknaps off lightly. His anger boiled to new heights: a jerk-off! A goddamn JERK-OFF! Not only YANKING his WANK, but with his OWN FINGERS at his BUNGHOLE! Well, not ONLY would he have to be punished!   He would be made an EXAMPLE of! Where this kind of flagrancy was concerned, Knighten thought furiously, what was good for the students would do for a TEACHER as well!

For a split second, the two men merely stared as each other: The burly salt-and-pepper commandant towering over the employee ten years his junior, seated on the toilet, pants and underwear at his ankles. On the one hand, there was no ques-tion that Belknaps was a man who kept himself in shape. He jogged and used the school gym regularly. He was well-formed, pleased with his 30" waist, visible pecs, and nicely muscled legs. Still and all he weighed only about 160 pounds, and was relatively short, only a little over 5'7"—hardly a match for his massive boss. Despite his thirty-five years, he was almost boyish, and certainly, at this embarrassing instant, he looked at the Commandant with an expression of almost childish terror, exactly as if he were one of the cadets "caught in the act." Not only was he deeply humili-ated to have been encountered in such a compromising position, not only was he pretty certain this would cost him his job, with this infuriated bear of a man before him, Ned could believe the Commandant capable of almost anything.

Still, he could not have IMAGINED what was in store for him!

"Come with me, Belknaps! NOW!" Knighten growled, grabbing the younger man by the ear and yanking him to his feet.

Belknaps struggled, but Knighten grasped his arm and twisted it behind his back. For Ned, it was like a dream... and soon to be a NIGHTMARE! His superior—resplendent in his uniform-- pulled him from the stall and across the tiled floor of the faculty men's room, and then before Ned knew it, they were OUT the swinging door and INTO the hallway!

Belknaps stumbled along, his arm pinned against his spine, the Commandant holding him firmly in front and to one side of him. Their progress was surprisingly rapid, given that both Ned's pants AND his underpants were still tangled around his ankles as Knighten propelled him forward.

"My God!" Ned thought in a blurred instant, "he's taking me back to my classroom!"

Sure enough, that was their destination. They continued down the cavernous corridor past the Commandant's office. The two cadets standing guard that hour at the office door, together with a couple just dispatched from inside with messages of one kind or another, looked on incredulously at the teacher with his pants AND his drawers down, being dragged along by the severe, uniformed Commandant. Half bent-over in some almost unconscious attempt at modesty, Ned could feel the cool air of the notoriously underheated school caress his flopping penis and testicles, and knew, as he was hustled past the boys, that his china-white, almost hairless behind must be SHINING like a BEACON in the dim light of the high-ceiled hallway.

For all the world, Ned Belknaps appeared to be nothing more than an obstreperous boy caught in some sort of naughtiness.

He felt blood rush to his face in shame.

"What's sauce for the goose in sauce for the gander!" Knighten rumbled as he thrust the helpless Belknaps before him.

Ned finally found his voice. His shock had been so great at what was happening, a full minute or more had passed as he had been unceremoniously escorted down the hall with his pants down.

"Mr. Knighten, you can't...."

"CUT YOUR BLUBBERING, BELKNAPS!" The Commandant roared. He was red with rage, veins swelling in his temples. As they reached the corner where the corridor turned, he halted. He pushed Ned slightly forward.

SMACK! SMACK! SMACK!

With his free hand, Knighten delivered three sharp SWATS to Ned's exposed posterior! "You'll be blubbering PLENTY before I'm done with you!"

He yanked him around the corner. The two boys bearing messages followed close behind, their duties momentarily forgotten This was simply too astonishing to be believed! Had they really seen the Commandant hauling a teacher down the hall, a teacher with his pants and underpants pulled down! Who was it? Mr. Belknaps! That new history teacher. And had the Commandant really just stopped, bent the teacher over, and administered three loud SPANKS to his bare behind?

Rounding the turn and closing the distance, there was no doubt about it. Three distinct, ROSY handprints bloomed on Mr. Belknaps' milky rear end!

The two teenagers glanced at each other, giggled in amazement, and quickened their pace.

The Commandant had no idea the two boys were following, nor that the office was without its honor guard as those two cadets took off in hot pursuit as well. At that moment, he would not have cared. He was BLIND with fury! From this outrage, a lesson would be learned by all!

They rounded another corner, and then--through the doorway and there they were. The thirty young men in class--hard at work on their Modern European History quiz--looked up, and, for a moment, were literally dumbstruck. There was their teacher, trousers and shorts around his ankles, his cock half-hard, and his round rump displayed, being dragged into the room by Commandant Knighten.

What was going on?

After the initial shock, a number of boys shot their hands

before their mouths to hide their blooming grins. My Lord! What were they to make of the sight of this authority figure in such an embarrassing situation? Toby Steele and Mike Green, in particular, could hardly contain themselves before Mr. Belknaps' HUMILIATING predicament.

Mr. Knighten tossed Belknaps easily across his own desk, so that the young men were treated to the sight of their teacher's plump fanny facing directly at them, white as snow, with three bright hand prints EMBLAZONED upon it. It didn't take much imagination to figure who had impressed those on their teacher's behind.

WOW!

As Knighten leaned hard against Belknaps' back ("OUCH!"), the younger man arched and his legs momentarily came off the ground and spread clumsily apart at the knees, exposing his lightly haired buttcrack and a hint of the wrinkled, brownish-pink pucker of his anus to his entire class.

"CADETS!" Knighten intoned loudly. "It is difficult for me to tell you this, but I encountered your teacher in an EXTREMELY compromising position in the faculty men's room. There is no need for me to explain to you our attitude at Brownsfield Academy toward the practice of self-pollution. You all KNOW what the punishment is for any cadet who is caught masturbating, though I'm not sure," he added roughly, "that Mr. Belknaps has been here long enough to know."

He punctuated his words, at that point, with a sharp SMACK of his massive palm to the teacher's naked buns. Another huge handprint blossomed on Mr. Belknaps' ass! A couple of the cadets jumped in their seats at the loud report.

"I want to show you boys that, in this institution, we make no distinctions when it comes to unacceptable behaviors. Masturbating is masturbating, no matter who does it. Selwyn!" he shouted.

"Yes, sir!" The small but muscular sophomore rose instantly from his seat and snapped to attention.

"Go down to my office and tell Sergeant Piece that I need

both 'The Corrector' and also 'The Facilitator!' Snap to it!"

"Yes, Sir!"

The boy skittered immediately out of the room.

The other cadets looked at one another in shock. Which of them DIDN'T know what the Commandant was referring to? "The Corrector" was the Commandant's dreaded oak paddle, half-an-inch thick and five inches wide, which has "kissed" the backsides of hundreds of wailing cadets literally thousands of times as they bent over with their trousers lowered to receive their requisite correction in the Commandant's office.

And "The Facilitator?" THAT was the Commandant's maple hairbrush, the one he used on the younger cadets instead of the paddle. Some claimed its sting was even WORSE than The Corrector's, especially since it allowed for a literal RAIN of swats on a cadet's exposed backside. And they all knew that it, as opposed to The Corrector, was only applied with the cadet, pants and underpants at his ankles, sprawled unceremoniously across the Commandant's knee!

WHAT were they to be witness to?

Belknaps himself could not BELIEVE what was happening. Here he was, with his naked behind facing an entire classroom of boys and young men of all ages. These were his students, for God's sake, and his boss was displaying his bare bottom, his privates, and his very puckerhole, to them all. These were boys who, hardly fifteen minutes before, had respected and, in some ways, feared him. He had never imagined that a little fun in the men's room would lead to this!

"Very well, Mr. Belknaps!" Mr. Knighten said loudly. "Having been caught in the act of self-abuse, you will be subjected RIGHT HERE to the punishment that Brownsfield Academy metes out to all those who are incapable of self control! Steele! Get up here. Restrain Mr. Belknaps in this position."

The fair-skinned, dark-haired cadet popped from his chair and went immediately to the Commandant's side. Six-foot-four and 195 pounds, the powerfully muscled football player was easily able to hold his teacher in place despite his struggling, though it was considerably more difficult for him to control the broad grin on his face and the notable bulge growing in his trousers. This was TOO rich to be believed!

"Now!" Mr. Knighten barked, "I believe all of you know how we deal here at Brownsfield with masturbators!" He turned to the blackboard, and picked up a piece of chalk. He then wrote, in large, block letters, "BOYS WHO MASTURBATE GET SPANKED!"

He turned back toward the classroom. There was a fair amount of barely restrained tittering behind cupped hands as the young men surveyed the scene before them: their thirty-five year old history teacher with his pants and underpants puddled around his ankles, bent across his very own desk in his very own classroom, held down by one of their classmates. Not only that! There was their teacher's naked posterior, round as an apple, facing the class in all its glory, four massive handprints in blushing pink apparent on that field of white, about to undergo a punishment they were all too familiar with-- and for BEATING OFF!.

It was hard for them all to keep from laughing out loud.

Finally, Toby, holding his teacher across the desk, could no longer restrain himself. A full-throated guffaw burst from his lips at the humiliation of a man who, moments before, he was afraid would flunk him. He looked at the bottom spread before him and his classmates, and simply could not contain himself— Mr. Belknaps SHOOTING A MOON at everybody! And NOT of his own volition!

His teacher writhed beneath him, but Toby held him firmly, laughing even louder in that his thrashing around caused Mr. Belnaps to expose even more of his ass and tight ballsac to Toby's amused classmates. God, the guys in the front row could probably count the hairs around his asshole!

As soon as Steele began to laugh, the other boys ceased to bite their tongues, and their merriment echoed throughout the room. What a moment! Their teacher caught PLAYING WITH HIMSELF by the Commandant, dragged WITH HIS PANTS DOWN down the hall, SWATTED with the Commandant's heavy paw, and about to be subjected to what they all knew would be their lot if they were found in his situation—the UNSPARING BLISTERING of his TOTALLY NAKED TAIL!

Mr. Knighten let the laughter ring out for some time. What the hell! As a Marine, he was fully aware of the POWER of humiliation! In the Corps, he himself had been the object of same many times, and subjected others to it as well. He was DETERMINED to embarrass this overgrown whelp in such a way that he would never even THINK of touching his cock again, at least during class hours. The Commandant almost had to smile to himself as he tried to imagine this faculty member trying to control his class after this incident. The boys would NEVER let the mouthy Mr. Belknaps forget what had happened to him.

Ned himself was speechless! He could not CONCEIVE the position Mr. Knighten had placed him in--there, before his class with his pants down, BARE BOTTOM!--about to suffer who knew WHAT embarrassment!. He looked at the blackboard, the legend "BOYS WHO MASTURBATE GET SPANKED" plainly apparent.

Oh, God!

Mr. Knighten turned to the helpless teacher held down by the towering student. "All right!" he said. "Now, while we're waiting, we're STILL going to undertake some discipline here. There's nothing I can't stand like the failure of SELF-CONTROL!" He reached into the chalk deck and pulled out the pointer that Ned used to indicate various capitals and troop movements.

Mr. Knighten swished the 3 foot stick, thick as a finger, menacingly through the air. "Until Selwyn gets back, for the beginning, this should work just FINE," he said threateningly. "Now, Steele, get Mr. Belknaps up from the desk and face him toward the blackboard."

The young man grabbed his teacher by his tie, while, just as the Commandant had done, twisting his arm behind his back. Belknaps' rump was momentarily covered by his shirt tail as he stood before the classroom. The young cadet spun him around to face the students. In that instant, Ned finally SAW the stunned, amused, DELIGHTED faces of the thirty uniformed boys of his Modern European History class. They were very obviously ENJOYING every MOMENT of this! In actually confronting their close-shaven, scrubbed, grinning faces, Ned Belknaps finally realized the HORRIFIC HUMILIATION he was being subjected to. He felt a little faint, and suddenly very hot as the blood rushed to his cheeks as he flushed a VIOLENT red before his assembled students.

Never breaking his grip, Toby turned his teacher slowly to face the blackboard with its grim and juvenile message in the Commandant's bold hand.

"Bend him over farther, Cadet!" Mr. Knighten barked.

Toby was only too happy to oblige. Still using the tie, he pulled his teacher's head toward the floor. As he did so, Belknaps' shirt rode up, and the boys could now see the back of their teacher's balls and the lower portion of his plump rump-cheeks.

The Commandant swung the pointer in the air with a notable "SWISH."

"Not as springy as the willow I had to cut when I was a boy," he growled, "but it will do."

He surveyed the class before him, seeking the boy who seemed the most amused by his teacher's predicament. His gaze lit on the glittering teeth of Mike Green.

"GREEN!" he bellowed.

"Yes, Sir!" the cadet responded, bouncing to his feet.

"Assist Cadet Steele in his duties."

"Yes, SIR!" Mike brayed delightedly.

He approached Toby, took Ned's other arm, and twisted it back as well. The teacher was now helplessly bent over before the class, in the grip of the two powerfully built students.

"Steele!"

"Yes, Sir!"

"Expose Mr. Belknaps' posterior!"

"Oh, yes, Sir!" the boy responded with unrestrained glee.

He SLOWLY raised his teacher's shirttail. For the boys

observing, it was like a curtain rising, as Ned's smooth, round BOTTOM came into view. His buttocks were nicely formed for a man of his age—each shaped like a ripe melon, dazzlingly white, separated by a deep cleft. From that cleft, soft hairs protruded slightly, but the cheeks themselves were silky as a teenager's.

"Posterior exposed, Sir!"

"Sir!" a voice suddenly interrupted.

It was Selwyn.

"Mission accomplished, Sir."

There in the doorway stood the cadet, in one hand the oak paddle, in the other the hardwood hairbrush. Behind him stood Sgt. Pierce himself—a lanky, country boy of 28 enlisted in the reserves, his face a study in astonishment.

"Very good, Selwyn!" The Commandant said. "Stand at rest till I call for you."

"Yes, Sir!"

Commandant Knighten faced the room. Thirty students. Very well.

"Cadets! To begin Mr. Belknaps punishment, he will receive thirty strokes with the pointer on his BARE BUTTOCKS! Sound off, right to left, in order, as they are applied, with number of stroke and name! Do I make myself clear!"

"Yes, Sir!" the class bellowed in unison.

"Very well!"

The Commandant positioned himself to Ned's right. He swished the pointer in the air again. It hissed viciously. Somehow, he found himself exhiliterated. This was what it MEANT to be A COMMANDANT!

He drew back his arm in a wide arc, and then:

SWISH-CRACK!

"OH!"

"One! Amundsen, Sir!"

SWISH-CRACK!"

"AH!"

"Two! Arkanian, Sir!"

SWISH-CRACK!

"Three! Burbage, Sir!"
SWISH-CRACK!
"NOO!"
"Four! Chen, Sir!"
SWISH-CRACK!....
"OUCH!"

Ned's horror at his humiliation was momentarily forgotten as the pointer whished through the air. The concentrated BURN of the makeshift cane was UNBELIEVABLE! With each lash, a LINE of FIRE erupted across his bared buttocks. He struggled against the tight grip of Steele and Green with every CRACK!, but the two together were far stronger than he. Helplessly, YELPS of protest and pain escaped his lips as the Commandant THRASHED his exposed bottom.

"Fourteen! Marxbury, Sir!"
SWISH-CRACK!
"IKE!"
"Fifteen! Newman, Sir!"
SWISH-CRACK!
"OW-WOW!"
"Sixteen! O'Neal, Sir!"

The Commandant could feel the pointer strain each time it landed across Belknaps' backside. He himself was more than familiar with the cane and its use. though he had never employed one in his disciplinary duties at Brownsfield Academy. Mr. Knighten, from long and varied experience, considered himself something of an expert on the subject of the male posterior AND its punishment. From his own growing up, from the hazings when he was in high school through his service in the Corps to the sizzling spanking he had administered just yesterday afternoon, he prided himself on a capacity to achieve the MAXIMUM amount of discomfort with each smack with the minimum amount of real damage. He could "read" a bottom like a field manual. To do so, of course, the butt must be BARE, so Knighten could monitor the redness, blistering, and swelling of the rump. Not to mention, of course, the EMBARRASSMENT it caused the miscreant.

NEVER must the skin be broken. For the Commandant and those he admired, that was a sign of blatant incompetence. As his cadets well knew, a spanking from the Commandant went ON and ON, as he drove the unfortunate malfactor into PAROXYMS of squirming, flopping, kicking, bouncing, jiggling, and, of course, tears.

SWISH-CRACK!

"OW-OW!"

"Twenty! Patino, Sir!"

Belknaps had what the Commandant knew as a "giving" backside, almost perfect for spanking—round, firm but with enough fat to it that it could absorb virtually ENDLESS punishment if properly applied. That Knighten had determined this not merely by observing the curve of the cheeks and the considerable depth of the crack as he had prepared to thrash it. He had come to this conclusion from the very feel of it against his hard palm when he delivered those three sharp POPS to it in the hallway, and the fourth here in the classroom. Belknaps' body may have matured in other ways, but, Mr. Knighten observed, he had retained very "boyish" buttocks. Indeed, with just a few swipes of a razor up that furred valley, it might be mistaken for the rear end of some sixth or seventh grader.

Of course, in good time, this tough Marine had plans to TREAT Ned Belknaps' bottom in PRECISELY the fashion a child of that age might EXPECT!

SWISH-CRACK!

"AAYYEE!"

"Twenty-three! Solakov, Sir!"

"YIKE!"

SWISH-CRACK!

"Twenty-four. Tatterline, Sir!"

The boys of the class were mesmerized, suspended still somewhere between SHOCK and amusement. With each SWISH-CRACK, a new mark appeared across their teacher's rear, with a few dropping down to cross his naked thighs. More than one cadet squirmed in his seat, imaging how the pointer would BITE into his own naked fanny. Certainly, Mr. Belknaps' echoing CRIES, the way he ROSE on his toes or bent his knees, how he CIRCLED his rump there HIGH in the air after each stroke--all were a good indication how much each one must HURT! By now, the Commandant was skillfully CRISS-CROSSING Ned's naked ass with the improvised switch, welts intersecting welts, so that it almost looked like he had accidentally sat on a waffle-iron!

SWISH-CRACK!

"OHWAH!"

"Twenty-six! Vasquez, Sir!"

SWISH-CRACK!

"AHH-YAH!"

"Twenty-seven! Zamboni, Sir!"

At the same time, what a sight! A TEACHER getting SPANKED by the Commandant! And for PLAYING WITH HIS DICK! Who would have IMAGINED such a thing could happen? There was not a boy present who had not cried in the Commandant's office, often as a result of a bad report on the part of an instructor. And now, here was one of those very instructors with his OWN pants down, his naked rear end DISPLAYED to them all, and in very obvious DISTRESS!

And, given that both The Corrector and The Facilitator were present, Mr. Belknaps' SPANKING was obviously FAR from over!

SWISH-CRACK!

"ARH-GAAA!

"Twenty-eight! Selwyn, Sir!"

SWISH-CRACK!

"OUCHOH!"

"Twenty-nine! Green, Sir!"

SWISH-CRACK!

"AHH-AH-OW!"

"Thirty! Steele, Sir!"

As the thrashing ended, the silence seemed deafening, broken only by Ned's dull moaning. His poor ass was in

FLAMES. He wiggled it still as if it were stung by an electric current, to Toby and Mike's considerable glee. Mike thought, to the boys at their desks, it must look like the movement of some sashaying schoolgirl tossing her tail, out to catch a horny cadet's attention!

The Commandant now approached to survey his handi-work. Before the boys' attentive eyes, he placed a huge paw on one of Ned Belknaps' pulsing cheeks, then allowed his hand to move casually over the rump and thighs, even into the CRACK itself, judging the rear end's condition. As his palm moved hither and thither, he nodded absently to himself—Good. Good. Warm to the touch. A little sweaty.

Knighten thoughtfully massaged and probed Ned's rump, poked and pinched it, grabbing a handful of the buttflesh in his grip now and then to increase circulation and encourage greater sensitivity. He knew full well a boy's behind could, with vigorous spanking, actually "numb up," obviating the whole point of the punishment. Though a study in red and white, Belksnaps' rear was only slightly swollen, and certainly able to take FAR more discipline.

"Steele! Green!"

"Yes, Sir!" the pair chorused.

"Place Mr. Belknaps across the end of the desk. HIS desk!" The Commandant emphasized.

The two beefy seniors wrestled the struggling teacher into the ordered position. The class now observed their teacher from the side, slung across the varnished wood of his desk.

"Vasquez! Chen!"

The squat Chicano and the willowy Asian freshman, one of the youngest in the class, popped from their seats.

"Yes, SIR!

"Cadets, remove Mr. Belknaps' trousers."

"Yes, Sir!" The two rushed forward, knelt beside their incapacitated teacher, and began to unlace his shoes.

"No need for that!" The Commandant barked. "Take his trousers off OVER his shoes. His underwear as well."

With some effort, the two young men pulled Ned's pants over his dark oxfords. Chen folded them neatly. Then, they removed his boxer shorts. Positioned as they were, Vasquez caught a strong whiff of sweat and burn from his teacher's welted bottom. It made him almost dizzy.

"Now, brace yourselves and pull Mr. Belknaps' legs apart!"

"Yes, Sir!"

The brawny Chicano wrestler had little trouble yanking Ned's ankle toward him, though this cost the slighter Chen some effort.

Stationed by the door, Sgt. Pierce and Selwyn observed Ned's new situation. On the floor were his black oxfords, rising from them his black nylon socks to mid-calf. Then there were his well-shaped legs, topped by the swell of his well-marked thighs and welted buttocks. Then his body fell away at a 45 degree angle over the desk. In this position, his rear-end was cocked slightly upwards. This, with his legs spread wide apart, allowed them an unobstructed view of his downy balls and the very tip of his penis dangling between his thighs, along with a tuft of hair that barely hid his anus.

Sgt. Pierce looked upon Belknaps' circumstance with a mix of wonder and sympathy. After all, after hours, though no one knew it, he himself had suffered at the hands of Mr. Knighten. He would have died if anyone were aware, or even suspected, but he himself—a 28 year old man--was nonetheless subject to the Commandant's discipline! There had been the little matter of the unfiled forms that had ended up costing Brownsfield a pretty penny two years back. Given the choice between the loss of his job or a sound paddling with The Corrector, Pierce felt he had had little choice. Down came his pants and his underwear as well, and over The Commandant's desk he went for his first spanking since he left home at 17.

And WHAT a spanking! The Commandant had left his taut, round and hairy countryboy can SMOULDERING as the price for his error, face and eyes RED as his REAR from pain and embarrassment.

Since then, he had become as INTIMATELY familiar as any cadet with both that oak monster and with The Facilitator as well. Though these boys didn't know it, thank God, his own backside was STILL stinging from a FIRM application of that maple hairbrush to his VERY bare posterior while slung across Mr. Knighten's lap less than 24 hours before. For a minor screw-up in the calendar, Pierce had found himself at attention before the Commandant at 6:30—trousers PUDDLED around his spit-shined shoes, GI skivvies to his knees—getting a thorough, ten minute dressing down for his carelessness. Then, it was across his superior's knee for a BLAZING session with The Facilitator.

Despite his efforts to control himself, Pierce's narrow but plump and richly furred blond backside had jumped HELPLESSLY up and down over the Commandant's lap as his toes tapped a SHARP and DESPERATE tattoo on the hardwood floor. His copious apologies for his mistake had been to no avail. Knighten had SPANKED the young sergeant till he was squirming and sniffling good, his fanny blushing EVER BRIGHTER and ROCKING back and forth and his underwear creeping toward his shoes as he wiggled, whined and whinnied.

One thing was for certain, where spanking was concerned, the Commandant was TIRELESS. Dressing for work this morning, Pierce had noticed in the mirror his behind was STILL red as a RIPE TOMATO!

After his punishment, he had had to stand at parade rest—pants and drawers as well around his ankles--in the corner of the office till the Commandant had finished his work around 8:00. Up to this point, he had been the only employee of Brownsfield Academy he knew of who got spanked by "the boss." Now, he had to wonder, though certainly, in his time here, he had never witnessed THIS kind of spectacle!

"Selwyn!" The Commandant bellowed. "Hand me The Corrector!"

"Yes, Sir!"

"CADETS!" That bellow again. "Line up behind Selwyn!"

The boys scrambled to obey his order as Mr. Knighten strode, the thick paddle beneath his arm like a swagger stick, to the side of Belknaps" spread behind.

"We will now begin the SECOND phrase of Mr. Belknaps' punishment!"

The Commandant placed the paddle against Ned's exposed buttocks, standing to his right, where, luckily, it was Chen who restrained the teacher's ankle. The stocky Vasquez might have been so bulky as to interrupt the proper swing.

"It was approximately 13:10 hours that I entered the faculty men's room. Hence, for his self-abuse and lack of self-control, Mr. Belknaps will NOW receive 110 swats of the Corrector on his bare posterior. I will administer the first 10, BRISKLY and VIGOROUSLY! Sgt. Pierce will administer the last 10, IN THE SAME FASHION! The intervening swats will be administered in sets of 3 by each one of you." He surveyed the file of students, noting the other athletes in the class. "Mr. Arkanian. Mr. Newman. Mr. O'Neale. Mr. Zamboni. Step forth!"

The quartet—the Armenian discus thrower and shotputter, the scrappy Jewish wrestler, the towering black basketball star, and the Italian hockey player—broke ranks and stood at attention.

"Gentlemen," Mr. Knighten said, "as you complete your duties, you will replace, in this order, Vasquez, Chen, Green, and Steele, so they may undertake their assignments!"

"Yes, Sir!" The four chorused.

"One further note, Cadets!" The Commandant added menacingly. "If, in my judgment, any of you do NOT go about your assignment BRISKLY and VIGOROUSLY, after this phase of Mr. Belknaps' discipline is complete, I will PERSONALLY lower your trousers AND undershorts RIGHT HERE AND NOW in order to demonstrate the meaning of the words 'BRISKLY' and 'VIGOROUSLY' on your OWN bare posterior before we proceed! DO I MAKE MYSELF CLEAR!"

"Yes, SIR!"

Arkanian, known to his fellows at "Furball" for the heavy

black hair that covered not merely his chest, crotch and legs, but his ass and back, stood behind Selwyn and Amundsen, sweat beaded on his forehead. He was profoundly nervous. A scholarship student whose dad worked in the local mill, he was always anxious to be well thought of and respected by his fellow cadets. It was not that he had any question, with his powerful arms and torso, he could fulfill the Commandant's orders to the letter. However, virtually from the first moment. Mr. Knighten had dragged his teacher with his drawers down into the room, he had been in an absolute LATHER of excitement. The sight of that white and helpless butt decorated with four massive handprint had put an unmistakable buzz in his balls, and every SWISH-CRACK of the pointer across those jiggling buns had made his beercan cock tick up another notch. Now, looking at that welted ass spread before him, the slightest pink of Mr. Belknaps' butt-hole peeking at him from the depths of his sparsely furred crack, Arkanian's dick swelled angrily in its full glory in his tight uniform. Why was he so turned on by all this? Was he QUEER or something? What if the other guys noticed! Or the Commandant! God, when he actually SWUNG that paddle and felt it CONNECT with Mr. Belknaps' ass, he might spew a dripping puddle in his pants right then and there!

Ned's horror as he listened to Mr. Knighten's instructions grew beyond any bounds he could even imagine. He was not only to get spanked IN FRONT of the boys, he was to be spanked BY the boys! What GREATER humiliation could a grown man possibly endure! Even putting that aside, how much more PAIN could his ass take? The thrashing with the pointer had left his cheeks BURNING, and their tenderness would make the paddling even worse! He faced the awful possibility he might not merely cry OUT, but actually CRY. The embarrassment of that would be indescribable!

The Commandant rubbed The Corrector against the welted cheeks of Ned Belknaps one final time, and then:

SMACK! SMACK! SMACK! SMACK! SMACK! SMACK! SMACK! SMACK! SMACK! SMACK!

The paddlecracks ECHOED in the room like automatic weapons' fire. Mr. Knighten did not pause between swats. He knew his mission here, and THAT was to reduce the obnoxious Mr. Belknaps to a wailing CHILD! He would make him bawl NOT like a maggot frosh cadet, but like that maggot frosh cadet's LITTLE SISTER! Then, in Phrase 3 (and Knighten had to bite his cheek to keep from grinning at the prospect), he would humiliate him utterly and completely.

"AAAHHHOOOOOOOUUUUCCCCHHHHAAAHHHOOOW WWWAAAAOOOHHHHHHHHEEEEEEEEOOOOOOOOOAAAAA RRRRRRRAAAHHHH"

The spanks fell so quickly on Ned's already BLAZING bottom his protests were unbroken, one constant HOWL of outrage and pain as his rear absorbed the oak's terrible STING. His rear end bounced SHAMELESSLY—up and down, back and forth--under the paddle as he strained against the grip of the four cadets restraining him. His balls and dick jiggled freely between his thighs.

"Selwyn!"

"Yes, Sir!"

"Pass The Facilitator to me."

"Yes, Sir!"

Knighten placed the mean-looking hairbrush on top of the desk, just beyond Ned's nose. Thus, when Belknaps opened his eyes, he would have to LOOK at it, and thus know, during his paddling, yet ANOTHER instrument of discipline awaited him afterwards!

The Commandant then passed the oak paddle to Selwyn.

"Cadet! Prepare to PUNISH!"

"Yes, Sir!" Selwyn shouted. The lanky auburn-haired swimmer lined up the paddle carefully right on the crown of Ned's buns. To assure his aim, he momentarily placed his left hand on the small of his teacher's back. Then, he drew back his arm.

WHACK! WHACK! WHACK!

"OW-WOW! OW! OUCH!"

"Very good, Selwyn. Amundsen!"

Now, it was the blue-eyed, blindingly blond Norwegian junior, a boarder and favorite among the "townie" girls.

WHACK! WHACK! WHACK!

"WOW! OUCH! OHHHH!"

"Arkanian!"

"Yes, Sir."

The sweaty cadet stepped forward, his boner literally bathed in lubrication against his underwear.

WHACK! WHACK! WHACK!

The hairy Armenian need not have fretted. He was far from alone in his excitement. There was hardly a dick in the class that was not at FULL ATTENTION as they approached the prospect of PADDLING their teacher's bare ass! Steele and Green had had hard-ons virtually from the first moment and, as the punishment had progressed, the other cadets had been HELPLESS before the effects of their raging hormones. Newman had to keep re-adjusting his trousers as his circumcised cock seemed to threaten to pop right out the buttons of his fly, while the pressure of the head of O'Neal's uncut black banger against his tight foreskin almost bent him over in discomfort. Though he had often seen the effects of a spanking on a whiteboy's rear, he had never actually watched a cracker ass get walloped, and it was QUITE an experience.

Boy, a honkie bootie got RED!

The thrill of the moment knew no boundaries, though, of race, religion, or creed--Kelly's Irish pecker and Tatterline's English prick, Chen's Asian penis and Dandorf's German pole, all were STONEHARD in their pants.

WHACK! WHACK! WHACK!

"OW! OUCH! AAAHH-AHHHH!"

"Eggbert!"

"Yes, Sir!"

Of all the boys, perhaps the most excited was Marxbury. This was not all that surprising. His bare five inches nestled against his lower belly, dripping with precum. Finally, he was getting the chance to see somebody else stripped and humiliated, rather than being stripped and humiliated himself.

Marxbury was himself a boarder, a junior, certainly not the smallest or weakest of the cadets. But he DID have the smallest dick. As a consequence, ever since his arrival at the Brownsfield barracks, he had been designated "house pussy." Such was the Academy tradition, passed down from class to class for decades, and, in all the years, the secret had never been betrayed. Neither Knighten nor any of his predecessors—not even most of the day students--had been privy to this informal arrangement among the randy boarders. Among them, he with the smallest cock was required to provide sexual service at "the designated hour"—from 4:00 to 5:00 a.m.—to any other boarding cadet, with no regard to rank or status. His mouth and asshole were at the "full disposal" of any who chose to visit his bunk.

Twenty years before, the story went, the "house pussy" had been the Commander of Cadets himself, now a Marine Corps colonel assigned to NATO in Brussels. By day, he supervised his fellows, prepared duty rosters, and imposed official sanctions. By night, rump high and nose low, he crouched naked on his mattress to await any cadet who wished to get a blowjob, have his ass kissed, or to fuck his commander up the rear.

WHACK! WHACK! WHACK!

"OW! OHHHH! AHHHH!!"

For three years now, this had been Marxbury's fate. With each new crop of boarders, he had hoped there would be one with a squatter cock than his own, but, when the tape measure came out for the secret "inspection" conducted in September, it was revealed he had once again "come up short."

WHACK! WHACK! WHACK!

"AAAHHHOOWWWEEEYYYYEEE!"

"Very good, Landsdowne. Larner!"

"Yes, Sir!"

Marxbury now had a clear view of his teacher's red rear. The way he was bucking around, you could occasionally catch a glimpse of his pinkish pucker. He wondered if Mr. Belknaps had ever had a dick up him. The way he was wiggling, it reminded Marxbury, embarrassingly, of the constant, elaborate, and humiliating descriptions from the other boys of how he himself squirmed when he was getting his ass fucked. With sweat rivering down between his teenaged buns, his own bunghole stung and ached. Chen, Kelly, and Vasquez had all stopped by the previous night to ream his rectum, while Amundsen had settled for a blowjob. It had been Chen's first time. Marxbury hated getting fucked by the freshman, and Chen had been so nervous Marxbury had had to suck his cock first under Kelly's watchful sophomore's eye. Not only that, he had had to lick out the Chinese boy's glassy smooth, sweaty asshole, just because that was Kelly's favorite and he told Chen he should see what it felt like. Beyond that, for a first-timer, that freshman had lasted longer than Marxbury would have expected up his ass. Frosh often blew their loads only a few strokes past penetration of Marxbury's tight anus.

Then, he had to get porked by Kelly after swabbing out his ruddy-furred crack with his tongue while Chen watched. How Kelly loved getting his freckled, Irish ass kissed, providing a running commentary to the other cadets as he sat on Marxbury's face—"Yeah, slut, clean me out! Service that crack! Get your lazy tongue inside me, asswipe! Sniff my stinkin' butthole! You're better than fuckin' toilet paper, Marxbury!"—to the point sometimes those waiting in line had to "shush" him. Not only that, Kelly REALLY enjoyed the feel of his cock popping through Marxbury's muscled rumpring--so much he kept pulling his dick out all the way so as to feel it slam through that sphincter again. Getting fucked by Kelly was like getting gangbanged by a dozen guys. They were hardly done with him before Vasquez was beside Marxbury's cot for his nightly ram. God, that Mexican was the horniest guy he had ever seen! Sometimes he fucked Marxbury twice in one night. His thick brown poker had almost rubbed him raw after the two prior fuckings, and his hole was gaping and sloppy with the Chicano's spicy studsauce by the time 5:00 o'clock rolled around!

"Marxbury!"

"Yes, Sir!"

Larner passed him The Corrector. Marxbury was struck with the weight of it in his hands. It WAS a heavy son-of-a-bitch. He then looked at Mr. Belknaps' blazing ass. WOW! Was it RED! You could still make out those welts from the pointer, straight and dark in that scarlet field the paddle had wrought.

And there was almost half the class to go.

Marxbury was determined his own pants weren't going to come down for doing a shitty job. He remembered two weeks before, when he'd been called on in class and hadn't known the answer. Mr. Belknaps had made him feel like a total dork, the asshole. Well, now, with his teacher's bare and helpless rear spread before him, it was time for PAYBACKS!

Marxbury grabbed the paddle's ample handle almost as if it were a tennis racket.

WHACK!

"AHHHHHHH----"

WHACK!

"AAAOOOHHHHH----"

WHACK!

"HHHAAAAEEEEEE!!"

Ned's rump was a flaming INFERNO! He had almost forgotten his SHAME at getting spanked by his students, his entire consciousness concentrated on the unbelievable BURNING in his butt. The barrage of smacks in sets of three had him BOUNCING around like a mad puppet, but he could do nothing against the iron grips of those restraining him. His mouth was open in a constant "O" of outrage as he HOWLED the sonic equivalent of his rear end's pain.

How much MORE of this could his ass TAKE?

"Very good, Marxbury. Nelson!"

Knighten was smiling broadly. He couldn't help it. He had spanked enough butt to know when the tears were coming, and Belknaps could not hold out indefinitely. He'd soon be bawling like a snot-nosed kid, which was EXACTLY what the Commandant intended. The conceited Mr. Belknaps reduced to a wailing little BOY by a bunch of high school students!

Then, it would be time for The Facilitator!

The hard-bodied and hard-cocked cadets continued the RELENTLESS blistering of Ned Belknaps' hindparts. Each seemed to draw strength from the boy before his whacks. The teacher sang the keening song of someone COMPLETELY beneath the rule of the paddle, oak and rump providing LOUD and ONGOING percussion to the melody

"AAYYEEEOOOWWWWEEEEEOHHHHHHH!!!"

WHACK! WHACK! WHACK!

Perhaps it was appropriate that it was Toby Steele who finally drove Ned Belknaps over the edge. It was Steele who had held him down from the first, and Steele who had noticed, from time to time, that hard-on in his teacher's crotch. As he swung The Corrector as hard as he could, though the young man did not catch it, The Commandant noted a slight change in pitch in Belknaps' HOWLING—higher, more desperate, with the unmistakable hiccough of a "WA" at the beginning.

He smiled more broadly. Crying! THAT is what he needed to bring this campaign to its triumphant close. Childish BLUBBERING. Real TEARS! If Pierce did his duty (and Knighten had little doubt the Sergeant KNEW what the price would be if he failed!), then he would have his snotty staff-member PRECISELY where he wanted him.

"....AAAHHH-WAAH!"

Steele stepped back. What a RUSH! He had never thought administering three smacks of a paddle could provide such stunning pleasure. His cock was absolutely SCREAMING in his drawers, his whole lower body SUFFUSED with a warm glowing. He looked at the helpless, thirty-five year old ass before him, red as a CHERRY!

Man, this class of cadets had done a JOB on Mr. Belknaps' butt!

"Sgt. Pierce!"

"Yes, Sir!"

"You will now administer the final ten swats of The

INCIDENT AT BROWNSFIELD ACADEMY

Corrector across Mr. Belknaps' bare buttocks!"

"Yes, Sir!"

Pierce stepped forward and studied Ned's blazing back-side. Jeez! In all the spankings he had witnessed, in all the spankings he had suffered, he didn't think he'd ever seen a rear so ravaged. Each of those young cadets had really gotten his money's worth! He almost felt sorry for the paddled teacher, but he certainly wasn't going to go easy on him. Commandant Knighten obviously had his plans here, and Pierce was all too aware what was expected of him. Christ, if he went too lightly, he might find himself in exactly the same situation as poor Belknaps, right here and now. And that was too embarrassing to even con-template! He would do his duty, without question or pause.

Pierce gripped The Corrector firmly. He drew the paddle back.

WHACK! WHACK! WHACK! WHACK! WHACK! WHACK! WHACK! WHACK! WHACK! WHACK!

"AAAEEEEOOOOHHHOWWWWEEEEYYEEOOO WWAAAAUUUUHHHHHOOOOOAHHHHH!!!!   WAAAAHHHH!! WAAAHHHHH!!!"

The Commandant's seasoned analysis had been correct. Sergeant Pierce's ten rapid-fire smacks with The Corrector had finally driven Ned Belknaps over the edge. He strained MADLY against the strong grips of the cadets who held him down. Newman lost his hold and went tumbling backwards as Ned's leg FLEW from his fingers and then FLUTTERED in the air for the last three swats. The pain is his ass was INDESCRIBABLE, as if a pan of BOILING WATER had been tossed over it. Had he stuck his finger in a wall socket, no greater amount of JUMPING and JIGGLING could have been produced. TEARS helplessly sprang to his eyes and began to run down his cheeks, and, in a haze of BURNING RUMP and HUMILIATION, SOBS escaped his lips even as the echo of the last paddlecrack died.

"AAAAHHHH!! WAAAHHHHH!!!"

Mr. Knighten grinned. NOW the TRUE and FINAL punish-ment of Ned Belknaps could begin. He knew this moment well.

When, at last, the bawling started, ANY male—regardless of age--was EXACTLY where you wanted him.

He strolled casually to the desk and picked up The Facilitator.

"Cadets! Release Mr. Belknaps!" he barked.

The four young men sprang back, but Ned, as the Commandant would have predicted, remained over the desk, dazed, blubbing steadily like a child. And that is what he was now. A soundly punished CHILD! Mr. Knighten had seen the phenomenon many times before. Belknaps had been BROKEN, pushed across a line, turned from a man into a SNIVELING BOY. How often had the stern Marine reduced his young charges—and others as well!—to such a state.

NOW, it was this sassy teacher's turn.

"Amundsen!" he bellowed. "Provide me your chair!"

"Yes, sir!" The blond cadet popped up and pushed his chair from his desk to the front of the classroom

Knighten then reached down and took hold of Ned Belknaps' ear. He pulled him to his feet slowly. The blubbering 35 year old rose docilely from the desk, precisely as Knighten expected. Without his even thinking, Ned's hands flew to his behind to CLAW and RUB his BLAZING backside. Insodoing, he pulled up his shirt to try and relieve that AWFUL burning of his behind, unconsciously exposing to the assembled students his cock—shrunk to a mere NUB in his bush—and his balls. The Commandant quite consciously turned Belknaps to face the class, so they would see his tear-stained face and his shriveled private parts. Let the criminal CONFRONT his punishers!

Dazed, stroking his palms over his battered buttocks, his vision watery and blurred, Ned saw indistinctly the GRINNING boys before him—the boys who had PADDLED HIS ASS. Even the shyest, like Chen or Hawkins, seemed to be showing his teeth in delight. In some part of his brain that could still somehow ignore the incredible BURNING in his rear, Ned Belknaps registered an EMBARRASSMENT that was beyond measure, one he had not known since he was a child and his own father had pulled down his pants and punished him in front of his friends. But this was FAR worse! STRIPPED and SPANKED IN PUBLIC! At 35 years old! Before people HALF his age! And not merely that, they had actually PARTICIPATED—holding him down and SMACKING his STRUGGLING REAR till he had been reduced to TEARS!

And they were SMILING!

A terrific SHAME welled within him; a deep BLUSH rose in his face. Helplessly, though he fought it, another SOB racked his chest and escaped his mouth.

"BA-WHUUHHHH!"

"CADETS!" the Commandant blared. "Now we will enter into the NEXT phase of Mr. Belknaps' punishment for his lack of self-control. Obviously and properly, you have now driven him beyond the limits of any manly self-discipline, and so now I will treat him appropriately—not as a MAN, but as a CHILD, one who has BLATANTLY indulged in childish acts. As you know, the Facilitator is used on the posteriors of the YOUNGER cadets among you, but it will now be applied, BRISKLY and VIGOROUSLY, to Mr. Belknaps BARE BOTTOM!

"I use that word with intention, Cadets. Here you confront nothing more than a boy's BOTTOM--one which demands DISCIPLINE! Remember this: When SELF-discipline is lacking, then DISCIPLINE must be imposed!" The Commandant paused. "Let this be a lesson to you ALL!"

With that, Knighten sat on the chair Amundsen had provided, and, leading him by his ear, easily turned Ned Belknaps across his knee. The pantless and still sniveling instructor's backside now faced his class—BLAZING red and, due to his position, slightly SPREAD so as to reveal not merely his RUDDY malemounds, but his NUTS and ANUS to the staring boys.

The Commandant waited for an instant, allowing the cadets to view at their leisure their teacher's quivering body, most especially, of course, his HELPLESS and TOTALLY EXPOSED hindparts. He knew 60 eyes—62 if you counted Pierce as well—were RIVETED on that battered behind, forming a memory that would NEVER be erased. Just to be certain, the strict, salt-and-pepper disciplinarian pushed Ned's head further toward the floor, while simultaneously inserting his one knee between his legs to spread the buns even wider. Let them see EVERY INCH of this man's most private place. Belknaps' asshole winked BLATANTLY at his former charges, a slim slit surrounded by dark and sweaty curls in the narrow white stipe of his buttcrack, which then gave way to the SCARLET, WELTED, BLISTERED hills of his BARE BOTTOM.

The Commandant twisted Ned's right arm behind him to hold him in position and raised The Facilitator HIGH into the air.

Poor Arkanian, at that moment, felt his cock begin to spasm. Seeing the wrinkle of Mr. Belknaps' rumpring had pushed him beyond endurance. He felt the honeythick stain of jockseed spreading on his pants. Oh GOD! If the other guys noticed, what would they say?

The hairy Armenian need not have worried. The boys were in a FRENZY of lust. Marxbury, in the second to the last row, unashamedly had his squatty dick out of his pants, pumping his spew all over his hand. Newman's probe was now so BLITHERINGLY out of control in his seat where he couldn't sit still, while Zaboni had his hand down his own trousers, running through his thick Italian bush, completely incapable of restraining himself any longer. O'Neal's uncut black banger was BURSTING. He tried thinking of anything— icing, gang warfare, his mother— to keep himself from cumming. Vazquez had already shot a load in his drawers and was well on his way to shooting another. God, tonight he was going to plow Marxbury at least THREE times. This Mexican pole needed HOLE!

THWACK!

The hairbrush landed resoundingly on Ned Belknaps' naked rear.

"WOO-WOUCH!"

THWACK!

Ned's rump arched and then recoiled.

"OHH-WAAH!"

THWACK!

Again the maplewood seared his scalded rump.

"YAA-AAHHAACCHHH!"

THWACK!

"AHHH-WAAAHHH!!!"

THWACK! THWACK! THWACK!

"OWWW! OOHHHH! WAAAHHHH! OWWW!"

Yes! thought the Commandant. That tell-tale "wa…"

THWACKATHWACK!

"WA-AAHH!"

Helplessly, Ned began to wiggle his bottom, and a pair of tears coursed down his cheeks as he hiccoughed a sob.

"BUU-AHHHHH!"

THWACK! THWACK!

Then another.

THWACK!

"WAA-AAHHH! AHHHH!"

THWACK! THWACK! THWACK!

"AAAHH-AAAHHHHH!!! WWAA--WAAHHH!"

THWACKATHWACK! THWACKATHWACKTHWACK!

"WA-AAHH!! AAAHH-AAAHHHHH!!! WWAA—AAHHH—WAAHHH!"

The Commandant smiled. Belknaps was TRULY beginning to CRY now. His body was twisting and straining slowly as his fanny shuddered FURIOUSLY. Mr. Knighten now knew how to proceed. With the HAIRBRUSH as his tool, the BARE BOTTOM as his means, he would DRIVE Ned Belknaps into a NIGHTMARE of JUVENILE and EMBARRASSING display!

The Commandant picked up the pace of the spanking.

THWACKATHWACKATHWACKATHWACKATHWACK!

"YAA-AAAHHH! BBUUU-WWAAA-AAHHH!! WAA-AAAHHHHH!"

Thanks to the STINGING fury of hardwood, he would propel Ned Belknaps into a FRENZY of humiliating and shameless self-abnegation! This masturbating, smart-alecky adult male would be transformed, before the cadet's eyes, into a kicking, squirming, wailing PUSSY of a brat across the Commandant's knee, an OBJECT LESSON in the POWER of SPANKING! To the end, the hardened Marine varied his technique, sometimes swinging his arm wide, sometimes merely flicking his wrist. With the hairbrush, even the SUBTLEST smacking thus produced could create an AWFUL and powerful BURN.

THWACK! THWACK! THWACK!

"WAAHHHH! AAA-AAAHHH!! BA-BA-BA-AHHHHH!!!"

Here, only the tip of the brush made contact; there, the entire wide face bore down on SQUIRMING rear as it QUAKED and SHIMMEYED. Like the military man he was, The Commandant engaged in a CONSTANT and HARRYING attack on Ned Belknaps' bottom—the HAIRBRUSH his sharpshooters, his infantry, his artillery, his PULVERIZING air power, all concentrated to transform this male backside into SMOKING, STEAMING field of PAIN!

THWACK! THWACK! THWACKTHWACKTHWACK!!!

"AHHHH! AAAHHHHH!! NNOOOOOO!! WAAAAA—AAHH-AAHHHHH!!! WWAAAHHHHHH!!!"

There was no turning back for Ned. Once those tears had erupted, he was HELPLESS. He forgot where he was. He forgot WHO he was. The spanking took him to some other space, some other time. He was no longer a grown-up. He was a youth, a lad, a boy, a baby—one who was turned over a MAN's knee, getting a good, old-fashioned, BARE BOTTOM SPANKING!

In that moment, one could have subtracted 30 years from his age. He was a mere 5 year old, getting his naked ass tanned but good! ASS? There beneath the hairbrush, his backside was not even a TEENAGER'S BUTT! The Commandant was right. It was a BOY'S BOTTOM, a FANNY, a HEINIE, a little brat's RUMPUS!

THWACKTHWACKTHWACK!!!

"AAAHHHHH!! WAA-AA-AHHHH!!! WWAAAHHHHHH!!!"

Ned strained against Knighten's firm grip, but it was hopeless. The Commandant had him exactly where he wanted him. Poised clumsily over the older man's knee, he could get no leverage. With his arm twisted behind his back, his movement was limited. Even more, ALL his energy seemed taken up in the FUTILE task of some avoiding, relieving, and somehow lessening just a WEE bit the TERRIBLE fire in his bottom! In that, of course, and his wild WAILING and WAAHING as he cried and cried. Ned wiggled his PUNISHED fanny SHAMELESSLY, engaging in a RIDICULOUS bump-and-grind before his young, amused, and FASCINATED audience.

THWACKTHWACKTHWACK!!! THWACK! THWACK!

"WWAAAHHHHH!! WAA-AA-A-AAA-AAHHH-AAAHHH!!!

Watching Mr. Belknaps' rear ROLL and WRIGGLE, Selwyn realized to his astonishment it most reminded him of his older brother's recent bachelor party. There, a sexy little "erotic dancer" had, to everyone's laughter, approached him and wiggled her steamy and bethonged ass right in his face! He had blushed five shades of red. But now, watching Mr. Belknaps' rump BOUNCE wildly over The Commandant's knee, that was all he could think of, his considerable penis poking painfully against his gut.

THWACKTHWACKTHWACK!!!

"AHHHH! UUUHHHHH!! WAAAAAHHHHH!!!"

Unwittingly, Ned's own "dancesteps" were evolving. As Mr. Knighten spanked him, his feet, at first, rocked back and forth on the toes of his shoes. Soon, however, again without his even thinking, they began to TAP helplessly on the floor, making a constant "rattatattatta" in a FRENETIC flamenco on the old boards of Brownfield Academy—softly at first, then gradually increasing in intensity and volume.

THWACKTHWACKATHWACK!!!

"YAA-AHHHH! BAA-UUHH-UUHHH!! WAAAAHHHH!!!"

Ra-ta-tatta-tattataata-RA-ta-tatta-tatta-RAT-TAT!

THWACKATHWACK! THWACK! THWACK!!!

"UUUHHHHH!! WAA-AA-AAHHHH!!! WAAAAAHHHHH!!!"

RATTATTATTATATTATTAT!

Finally, though, his oxfords rose slowly from the floor into the air.

THWACK! THWACK! THWACKTHWACKTHWACK!!!

"AHHHH! NO! AAAHHHH!! WAAAAAHHHH!!! WWAAAHHHHH!!!"

At first, his nicely muscled, lightly haired legs waved lazily as two tree limbs in a breeze.

THWACK! THWACK! THWACK!!!

"WAAAAAHHHHH!!! WWAAAHHHHHH!!!"

Then, Ned's legs began to pump up and down. Slowly at first.

THWACKTHWACKTHWACK!!!

"BU-BU-AHHHH! AAAHHHHH!! WAAAAAHHHHH!!!"

Then faster. Faster...

THWACKATHWACKATHWACK!

"WAAAAAHHHHH!!!"

Faster still!

THWACK! THWACK! THWACKATHWACK!!!

"WAAAAAHHHHH!!! BBUUHH-AAAHH!!! WWAAAAHHH!!!"

Ned's oxfords SHIMMERED now in a fantastic, frantic, girlish FLUTTERKICK! His free arm CLAWED the air. His head SNAPPED up and down. It was almost as if he were trying to SWIM through air, there held across The Commandant's lap.

THWACK! THWACK! THWACKTHWACKTHWACK!!!

"AHHH! AAAHHHH!! WAAAAAHHH!!! WWAAAHHHHH!!!"

His legs began to beat rapidly in wide arcs, his shoes a blur before his mesmerized audience. His ROILING rear end bounced WILDLY over the older man's knee as he was soundly SPANKED! His torso twisted from side to side, but Mr. Knighten held him firmly, smacking that butt ever HARDER and FASTER. Ned's head JERKED with every swat, tears STREAMING down his cheeks, his mouth in constant wide GRIMACE, an open "O" of pain and outrage, his crying now the high-pitched SOPRANO SOLO of a small child getting his bare behind THOROUGHLY and UTTERLY blistered! He wiggled as if his EXPOSED BACKSIDE were under attack by a swarm of ANGRY WASPS, each STINGING his BLITHERING BOTTOM again and again.

THWACKATHWACKATHWACKATHWACK!

"WAAAAAHHHHH!!! WWAAAHHHHHH!!!"

Mr. Knighten loved the Facilitator. Even more than the Corrector, it allowed him to literally RAIN smacks down on a hapless rump in an endless TORRENT of FIRE! Methodically but with great speed, he covered every INCH of the NAKED BEHIND held across his knee. NOW the fleshy crown of the rear, NOW at that most TENDER place where thigh meets buttock, now UP TOWARD THE WAIST, NOW to ONE SIDE, NOW to the OTHER. How WELL he knew the male posterior! And how well he knew, with the hairbrush, how he could deliver FOUR blows before the first had even registered, so the bottom was an entire CONFUSION of FLAME.

THWACKATHWACKATHWACKATHWACK!

"WAAAAHHH!!! AHHH!!! PLEEAASE!!! WWAAAHHH!!!"

Ned's legs now began to move not merely up and down, but BACK and FORTH as well. With no pants or underpants to restrain them, they SCISSORED wide apart in the air, exposing both his CRACK and HOLE. His ANUS was like a blinking PINK PANIC LIGHT facing the staring cadets, signing his ABSOLUTE distress! That MOST SECRET of malespots, hidden away between the rumpcheeks, was COMPLETELY exposed to PUBLIC view. Not only that, but it was Mr. Belknaps himself, unable to control his FLYING FEET as they spread wide and snapped shut, who was actually SHOWING OFF his very own RUMPRING to his very own students as he was getting SPANKED!

The boys were oddly quiet, completely hypnotized by the scene, the BLAZING buttocks, the BLOOMING butthole, the HOWLING man-turned-boy—stunned and amazed. Steele and Greene, despite their broad grins, were rooted to their desks, their DICKS directing their eyes toward that FLAMING, FLASHING, FLAILING rump. They could not keep their hands from their crotches. They rubbed their pants BLATANTLY.

THWACKATHWACKATHWACKATHWACK!

"PLEEEAAASEEEE!!! WWAAAHHHHHH!!! AHHHH!!! WAA-AA-AAAHHHH!!!"

Meanwhile, the Commandant SPANKED! In his task,

he was inexhaustible, playing Ned—most particularly his naked backside--like a fiddle, a drum, an entire BAND. Angry BLISTERS rose on the crown of the JUGGLING behind, slight, purple BRUISES appeared at the CREASE of rump and thigh. Belknaps SQUEALED and SQUALLED, he HOLLARED and HOWLED, he WAILED and WHINNEYED. His feet flashed in a FANTASIC FANDANGO, the footwork of a FRENETIC lapdance where the Commandant and his hairbrush called the tune. For the boys, it was a spectacle of UTTER power—Mr. Knighten the MASTER of Ned Belknaps, employing his NAKED bottom as the means by which to exercise his COMPLETE CONTROL.

THWACK! THWACK! THWACK! THWACK!

"YAAA-AAAHHH-WAAA-AAAHAAAHHHHH!!!"

And Ned? Ned was OUT of control—squirming, wiggling, yawing, kicking, bucking, bouncing, shaking and shuddering. His entire being was now concentrated on NOTHING but the unspeakable BURNING in his BOTTOM. It was as if real FLAMES were licking at his meaty buns, SCORCHING them SAVAGELY, SEARING them HELLISHLY hot! Sweat poured from his body as he thrashed like a BEACHED FISH over Mr. Knighten's knee, his RAVAGED RUMP the FOCUS of his entire consciousness, the CENTER of his universe--the very portrait of a WELL-SPANKED BOY.

THWACK! THWACK! THWACK!

"WAAA-AAAHAAAHHHHH!!!"

Sgt Pierce felt a deep flush rise in his face. He had never witnessed anything so TOTALLY and INTENSELY humiliating. His heart went out to Ned Belknaps, and, yet, he realized too his countryboy cock was stiff as a pike and ACHING in his pants. Despite his sympathy for the unfortunate teacher, there was something overwhelmingly AROUSING about watching those NAKED, BLAZING buttocks DANCE and LEAP across the Commandant's knee as the hairbrush did its BLISTERING work, seeing those feet FLY through the air, hear Ned's HOWLS and WAILS. He dragged his eyes from the spanking for a moment, and realized the cadets themselves were as well in a FROTH of sexual excitation. Some even had their dicks out of their pants!

O irony! Here was someone being PUNISHED for masturbating as boys OVERTLY played with themselves as they observed his public penance!

THWACKATHWACKATHWACKATHWACK! THWACK! THWACK! THWACK!

"PLEEEAAASEEEE!!! WWAAAHHHHHH!!! AHHHH!!! SIR! PLEAASSEE!!! WAA-AA-AAAHHHH!!! NNOOOO!!! AAAHHH!!! WAA-AA-AAAHHHHHHH!!!"

Kelly, his zipper half unzipped, diddled the head of his sloppy dick as he observed the show. He didn't know if anything he had ever witnessed had turned him on so completely, not even getting his asshole licked or ramming his poker up Marxbury's tight shitchute again and again. As one of 8 kids of a spanking Irish dad, he was no stranger to blistered behinds, male and female. During the summer, he often felt the bite of his father's razor strop there with his drawers down along with his brothers. His dad never spanked but on the bare. Still, the boys went over the back of a chair for their punishment. It was his sisters with skirts upraised and panties down he had seen across his father's knee for an application of that callused palm. And that, to him, was what Ned Belknaps looked like—a GIRL, kicking her legs over daddy's knee. What a WUSS! In that position, and BAWLING like a BABY! Kelly couldn't help smiling. At least he and his brothers maintained SOME kind of manly dignity as they took their strokes, but here was his teacher, wiggling and wailing across The Commandant's lap like some naughty little bitch!

THWACKATHWACKATHWACKATHWACK!!!

"SIR! PLEAASSEE!!! WAA-AA-AAAHHHH!!! NNOOOO!!! AAAHHH!!!"

Kelly was not alone in his observation. Watching Ned Belknaps DANCE and CRY over Mr. Knighten's knee as The Facilitator EXPLODED again and again on his BARE and BUCKING behind, lust was not the only emotion awakened within the cadets. Through the switching with the pointer and the paddling with The Corrector, many had felt a certain identification and sympathy for their unfortunate instructor. After all, each one had known the PAIN and SHAME of discipline by The Commandant.

Now however—seeing those feet FLY frantically through the air, that rump jump WILDLY up and down, listening to that unbroken BLUBBING as that bottom was thoroughly THRASHED—not only was their lust excited, but also emotions of AMUSEMENT, even CONTEMPT! There was something undeniably FUNNY about this entire scene. A FULL-GROWN man in such a JUVENILE position! His plump, round RUMP completely NAKED before them, DRIBBLING and BOUNCING like some human basketball, HELPLESS across a strict disciplinarian's lap, CRYING his EYES out, his legs FLAILING the air! Just a 35 year old teacher getting an OLD-FASHIONED, OVER-THE-KNEE, BARE BOTTOM SPANKING in front of his class!!

THWACK! THWACK! THWACKATHWACK!

"AAA-AAAHHH-WAAA-AAAHAAAHHHHH!!!"

"Not such a hotshit NOW, are you, teach!" Landsdowne muttered to himself while kneading his spuming pole against his thigh, stroking and even striking his cock as he watched and spoke unthinkingly.

"Spank him HARDER!" Selwyn whispered to himself as his hands moved, without his even realizing it, over the tight trousers that encased his own fevered dick.

"Flops around like a fuckin' fairy!" Zamboni whispered heavily to Vazquez, who nodded, his own gaze locked on Ned's straining butthole. He was deep into imagining how that sphincter would feel strangling his hot Chicano cock as he PORKED that FLOUCING fanny. Even the normally reserved Amundsen smiled broadly in the front row, his white blond pubes soaked with sweat and spunk, while Newman was possessed of nervous, helpless giggles, circumcised probe weeping drop after copious drop of shimmering pre-cum.

THWACK! THWACK! THWACK!

"PLEEAAASEEE!!! YA-AA-AAHHHH!!! WWAAAHHH!!!"

O'Neale leaned back in his seat, his black probe well

on its way to its THIRD explosion. "Jeez, white boys DO carry on!" he thought, "No matter HOW big they get." Still, he was astounded, on some level. Who would have though ANY whiteboy could perform that kind of JIVE and JITTERBUG! He watched Mr. Belknaps' bootie BOUND and BOUNCE, driven by that hairbrush to a kind of ROCKIN' RHYTHM that would have made ANY black boy proud. And that was sure some fancy FOOTWORK, his teacher's shoes hip-hopping toward the sky as the Facilitator BLASTED that butt again and again. Maybe all any honkie-boy needed was a little BARE BOTTOM encouragement from a TRUE STUD to get rhythm!

THWACK! THWACK!

"PLEEEAAASEEE!!! WWAAAHHHHHH!! NNOOO!! AAHHHHHH!!"

Steele and Greene, of course, in PAROXSYMS of delight, had huge SNEERS painted on their faces at the spectacle before them, sneers HARD as their THROBBING dicks. They were filled with admiration at the BLISTERING Commandant, wishing the both of them that THEY were the ones administering this COMPLETE and completely HUMILIATING SPANKING! Those WILDLY WINDMILLING legs, that HAWING, HEAVING chest, AND, of course, that BLAZING, BUCKING BOTTOM! What sight could be SEXIER, in the end, than this one of TOTAL and TERRIBLE dominance!

THWACKATHWACKATHWACKATHWACK!!! THWACK! THWACK!! THWACKTHWACK—THWACKATHWACK!!!

"AYYYYEEE! OWWWW!!! OOOOHHHHHHHH!!!! WAAAAAHHHHHH!!! AAAHHH-AYYYYEEE!!! BU-UU-AAAHHHH!! WWAAAHHHHHH!!!"

Still, Mr. Knighten THRASHED those madly moving male-mounds, the Facilitator grasped firmly in his hand, drawing strength from each echoing THWACK! The hairbrush, like some smart-bomb, EXPLODED endlessly across Ned Belknap's BEHIND, carpeting those SMOKING buns with NEW and TERRIBLE fire, INCINERATING that fanny like a FLAMETHROWER.

THWACKATHWACK!!! THWACK! THWACK!!

"OOOOHHHHHHH!!!! WAAAAAHHHHH!!!"

And Ned? His CRAZY CAN-CAN continued, his toes never touching the floor as shoes drew crazy SQUIGGLES and CIRCLES in the air, his rump WRIGGLING and WRITHING rhythmically beneath the hardwood blasts that ROCKED and RAISED his rear there across the Commandant's knee. As if SCOURED with STEAM, Ned's BOYISH BUNS were now BURNING, BLAZING PYRES of BLISTERED BUTTFLESH!

THWACK! THWACK! THWACK!

"WA-AAAAHHH! WAA-AAA-AAHHHH!"

THWACKATHWACK!!! THWACK! THWACK!!! THWACK!!!

"YAA-AAHHH!! OOOHHH!!! AAAHHHHHH!!"

As the punishment continued, the very atmosphere of the room was transformed. Ned's HOWLING cries and the INCESSANT percussion of the HORRIFIC HAIRBRUSH on his HUMPING heinie filled the room, REFLECTING off the CEILING and BOUCING off the walls! His FRANTIC, HIGH-PITCHED BAWLING seemed to grow even LOUDER as it BILLOWED and BLARED through the door and down the halls of Brownsfield Academy.

THWACK! THWACK! THWACKATHACK!

"WAA-AAA-AAHHHH! AAAHHHHHH!!! OOOOOOOOO!! BBUUU-HHAAHHHH! YAAA-AAA-AAAHHHHHH!! WAA-AAHH-AAAHHHH-AAAAHHH!!"

For the cadets, the very AIR they breathed seemed heavy with the unmistakable SCENT of SPANKING—HOT male sweat and even HOTTER skin, of ASSHOLE and BUNS at BROIL, mingling with the distinctive aroma of males in full RUT! MUSKY and ACRID, FANNED by the FLAILING brush, it filled the nostrils of the cadets and INCREASED, if that were possible, the LUST of their LOADED mantools. It was almost as if their TONGUES could TASTE that smell wafting toward them, the FLAVOR of a FLOPPING FANNY set squirming MANICALLY by the UNFORGIVING force of a DETERMINED DISCIPLINARIAN!

THWACK!THWACK! THWACK! THWACKATHWACKA

THWACK! THWACK!

"WA-AAAAHHH! WAA-AAA-AAHHHH! YAA-AAHHH!! OOOHHH!! WA-AAAAHHH!!!!"

Still spanking, The Commandant's mind was already racing forward. As a seasoned spanker, he was already considering his options in FURTHER humiliating the WAILING miscreant struggling WILDLY across his knee. His arm implacably ROSE and FELL as he weighed the possibilities, a STRICT MAN utterly COMMITTED to his DUTY to SPANK and SPANK and SPANK SOME MORE!

T H W A C K A T H W A C K A T H W A C K A T H W A C K ! ! ! THWACKATHWACK!!!

"AYYYYEEE! OWWWW!!! YYAAAAAHHHHH!!! AAAHHH-AYYYYEEEE!!!"

Finally, Mr. Knighten knew his next move. He gradually slowed the rhythm of his smacking.

THWACKATHWACK! THWACK!

"AHHHHH!!"

THWACK!!…

"YAA-OOHHH! WWAA-AA-AHHH!!"

THWACK!!!……

"WAA-AAA-AAAHHHH!!! WAA-AA-AAHHHH!!"

Then, with six sudden, powerful, rapid SWATS—THWACKA THWACK THWACKA THWACKA THWACK THWACK!!!!

--the hairbrush stopped its constant motion.

The room still reverberated with Ned Belknaps' BLUBBERING howls!

"WAA-AAA-AAAHHHH!!! BUHUH-UUHH-AHHHHH!!! WAAA-AAA-AAAHHHHH!!!"

But, for a moment, the spanking had ceased.

The Commandant, calmly, let The Facilitator drop to the floor with a sharp "TAK!"

The cadets, to a man, let out a collective breath. Was this punishment FINALLY at an end?

Even if it were, Ned's BAWLING continued unabated--"WAA-AAA-AAAHHHH!!! WAA-AAAHHHH!!—as his flaming fanny quailed and quivered over the Commandant's lap.

And then, Knighten shifted the position of helpless teacher. He thrust his other knee between Belknaps' legs, so the blazing buttocks were splayed as WIDE as they could possibly be. Thus, Ned Belknaps' balls and the tip of his prick were in full view of all, hanging free between the Commandant's legs. The narrowest band of white split the field of red from the waist to those dangling nuts. As Ned's bottom still helplessly WAGGLED, spreading open and snapping shut, the cadets in the front row could see even beyond his wrinkled pucker to the pure pink of his spasming rearhole.

"Now, Mr. Belknaps," the Commandant intoned, "we will COMPLETE the administration of your punishment. You will do as I tell you. Do you understand?"

With that, the Commandant raised his arm, and brought his palm down DIRECTLY on the FULLY SPREAD ANUS before him.

SMACK!

"ACK! YES! YES!" Ned wailed.

SMACK!

"That is 'Yes, SIR!' Do I make myself clear, Belknaps!"

SMACK!

"YE-WOUCH! YES, SIR! YES, SIR!" Ned Belknaps warbled wildly.

Now, he would do anything he was told. ANYTHING to stop the burning in his bottom! What difference did it make anyway? He had been TOTALLY CONQUERED. He was CRYING. He was KICKING. He wore NO pants or underpants. He was TURNED ACROSS a MAN'S KNEE. His BACKSIDE was ON FIRE. He had been THRASHED within an inch of his life. The Commandant had turned him from a grown man into a BLUBBERING, BUCKING, BAWLING little BOY! And this, in front of THIRTY-ONE WITNESSES—young men who would NEVER forget what they had seen, and would never let HIM forget! And now, his boss was slapping his ASSHOLE—spread WIDE for all the world to see! He had been SPANKED into utter submission. What FURTHER degradation could he endure!

"Very well," the Commandant growled. "Repeat after me Belknaps…"

SMACK!

"AHHHH!"

"BOYS!"

SMACK!

"OOWWW! BOYS!"

SMACK!

"WHO!"

"ACCKK!" Ned howled. "WHO!"

"MAS--!"

Oh my God, Sgt. Pierce thought, he's making him ANNOUNCE what he's getting spanked for!

"AHHH!" Ned's legs rose simultaneously into the air as the Commandant's palm connected with his tender perianum. "MAS!"

"TUR--!"

SMACK!

"AYIII! TUR!"

"BATE!"

SMACK!

"AW-WAAH! BATE!"

"GET!"

SMACK!

"WAA-AAAH! G-G-G-ET!"

SMACK!!

"SPANKED!!"

SMACK !!

"AAHH-WAAAHHH !! SP-SP-SP-SPANKED !! WAA-AA-AAHHH!!"

At this moment, the Commandant himself seemed to enter into some kind of trance. His arm flew in the air, again and again, his hand SNAPPING against the SQUIRMING SEAT of Ned Belknaps, the palm striking loudly in what seemed an IMPOSSIBLY rapid rhythm, all the while repeating: "Boys who masturbate get SPANKED! Boys who masturbate get SPANKED! Boys who masturbate get SPANKED!" Knighten roared out the message to the DRUMMING, CRACKING resonance of skin on skin. SMACK! SMACK! SMACK! He was hypnotized by the task before him, removing that last white from Ned's behind, leaving the space below his bunghole, the crack, the pink hole itself FLAMING red and SWOLLEN as those round mounds of the man's flailing fanny.

SMACK! SMACK! SMACK!

"OWWW! AHHHH! WAAA-AAHHHH!!!"

Given this, he did not notice that the tattoo he beat on Ned Belknaps bare buttocks matched the marching time of fingers on cadet COCK! Every boy in the room now had his hand to his crotch—stroking, tickling, rubbing. Not only Marxbury had his fly completely open, yanking wang to the sharp report of spanking. Others had their hands completely down their pants, cradling bursting balls and fingering their swollen members. Still others simply passed their palms wildly over the front of their trousers, as the peaks of their probes, helpless, pushed against and sometimes even escaped the tight waistbands of their pants, dickheads weeping male honey on the stomachs of their shirts. Even Sgt Pierce, utterly other than himself, was blatantly rubbing his fly, his backwoods pussybanger leaking country gravy that soaked through his drawers and stained the front of his uniform pants.

SMACK! SMACK! SMACK!

"AAIIIAAAYYYAAAWWWAAAAHHHHAAAHHHAAAHHH HH!!"

Shy young Chen was, with the best of them, playing with his throbbing Asian pecker. He had never imagined he would EVER witness something like THIS. What a SPANKING!! And of a full-grown man! Not only that, he was certain, as he watched the blur of The Commandant's massive paw strike Mr. Belknaps' rear again and again—could it be? YES! He saw it again! The very tip of Mr. Knighten's fingers was actually ENTERING the teacher's butthole! Mr. Belknaps was not only getting a

SPANKING, he was getting publicly FINGERFUCKED! He could see his teacher's butthole GRIPPING the Commandant's thick digit. He recalled how Kelly, the night before, had had him stick his finger up Marxbury's ass before he fucked him ("See how tight it is? Wait'll you feel that on your DICK!"). This was AMAZING!

SMACK! SMACK! SMACK!

"WWWAAAAHHHHAAAHHHAAAHHHHH!!!"

Chen was not alone in his observation, nor was he incorrect. Beneath the Commandant's unforgiving assault, Ned's behind was slick with greasy sweat. As he bounced about, particularly from certain angles, the Marine's hairy paw struck in such a way that, indeed, it actually violated the lubricated ring of the spanked man's bunghole.

SMACK! SMACK! SMACK!

The slap of a man's hand on his bottom might have been, some time before, bearable for poor Ned. But now, his rumpus RAVAGED by the pointer, the paddle, and the brush, the Commandant's palm was as fiery as a WHITEHOT frypan. His BABYISH SHRIEKING filled the room, his widely spread legs PUMPING madly, his ass as red as MARS—the planet of WAR—and PULSING, QUIVERING, QUAKING! As his punishment had continued, he had been forced ever further over The Commandant's lap. His nose now rested on the floor. Mr. Knighten no longer bothered to hold his arm. Ned's fists now beat the floor frantically as The Commandant beat his SPLAYED and SUFFERING rump! It was as if Mr. Knighten had SPREAD HIS ASS and released an ARMY of ANTS to BITE and BORE into his AGONIZED ANUS.

SMACK! SMACK! SMACK!

"WWWAAAAHHH-HAAAH-HHAAAHHHHH!!"

And WHAT a sight that anus presented for those boys in the first row! It no longer appeared the slim slit of a male shitchute. With the repeated CRACKS of The Commandant's hot palm across it and its ongoing rough INVASION by the finger, Ned's pucker now more resembled a PULSATING PUSSY—teasing, begging, demanding a deep and extended SHAFTING by a stiff and manly DICK! The asslips swelled ANGRILY in a tight, throbbing ring that could only be soothed by the massage of PROBING cock, which, at that moment, any ONE of the cadets would and could have GLADLY provided!

SMACK! SMACK! SMACK!

"YYYAAAAHHH-HAAAH! AHHHH-HHAAAHHHHH!!"

From somewhere from deep in his memory, Ned could hear himself, back when he was 12, 8, 5, from when he had mis-behaved and his angry father had had to pull down his pants and discipline him "GOOD and HARD," some words that had made the TERRIBLE pain in his naughty boy's fanny STOP! Some half-lost recollection surfaced dizzily. In the midst of his squeal-ing, he somehow found his voice.

"PLEASE!!" Ned squealed. "SIR! PLEASE!! WA-AA-AHHH!!! I'LL B-B-B-BEEE... AAAHHH!!! WAAAAHHH!!! A-A-A G-G-G-G-GOODDDD!!! WA-AA-AAAHHHH!! B-B-B-BOOOYYY!!!! YAAA-AAA-AAHHHH!!"

SMACK! SMACK! SMACK!

Mr. Knighten's hand continued its RELENTLESS whack-ing.

SMACK! SMACK! SMACK!

"YYYAAAAHHH-HAAAH! AHHHH-HHAAAHHHHH!! SIR!! BUU-HAAAHHH!! DADDY!! OOWWWW!!! I WILL!! WA-AHHHHH!!

SMACK! SMACK! SMACK!

"AAAAHHH-HAAAH! WWAA-AHHHH-HHAAAHHHHH!! DADDY!! NOOOO!! BAAHHHH!!! A GOOD...! WAA-AA-AAHHH!!! B-B-B-BOY!! YA-AAA-AAHHH!!"

SMACK! SMACK! SMACK!

Ned Belknaps' wailing pleas somehow penetrated the tough Marine's consciousness. YES! THIS is what he had want-ed to hear. This smart-aleck BEGGING! Calling him DADDY! Calling his very SELF a BOY!

But did the Commandant STOP the spanking? NO! His cracking palm REDOUBLED its assault on Ned's BROILING bot-tom, and Ned's PATHETIC PLEADING rose to even GREATER

were splayed wide apart. Now, no spot of white interrupted the field of FLAME that lit his body from the top of his thighs to his waist, from hipbone to hipbone, all down the asscrack, around the anus to the peak of his ballsac. Across his rump, BLISTERS rose in dots of white, and here and there a dark BRUISE showed through the reigning SCARLET. Though the SPANKING had stopped, he continued to JIGGLE helplessly across the older man's knee, his butthole SQUEEZING and then RELEASING the hairy digit of The Commandant, planted up to the third knuckle DEEP in his rectum.

Suddenly conscious of themselves, the cadets as one man realized the punishment was apparently over. There was a rapid, almost frantic readjustment of clothing as throbbing spunky dicks were stowed back in the confines of their tight trousers. After what they had just witnessed, who among them wanted to even THINK the word "masturbate!'

Without a word, Mr. Knighten began to raise his hand slowly upward, maintaining his finger in its position. Responding inevitably to the pressure within him, Ned Belknaps was pulled to his feet, though still bent over. For those observing, it was like watching a RAGING red sunrise. Or, perhaps, a MOONrise, as those FIERY globes were lifted off Mr. Knighten's knee. The Commandant grasped the collar of Ned's shirt to steady him. Belknaps was now truly the older man's puppet, his FINGER puppet. He controlled Ned's every move. As he pulled him to his wobbling feet, Knighten made sure to poke the younger man's prostate, so that he helplessly wiggled his roasted rear at his audience like some seductive slut, just as The Commandant intended.

But that was not his ONLY intent. Mr. Knighten knew the male posterior both outside and IN! He was quite aware of another effect his rough probing of Ned Belknaps' most sensitive and hidden spot would achieve. If the SPANKING of this mas-turbator was at an end, his HUMILIATION most CERTAINLY was NOT!

Sure enough, though Ned, of course, could have no

knowledge of or control over it, something ELSE began to rise at the sensation of The Commandant's hot palm against his brutalized behind and, more especially, that of his anus on the Marine's probing digit, the tip of which, there inside, was unmercifully flicking his ticklish man-gland. Mr. Knighten paused a moment, GRINDING his nail against the soft, hot wall of Belknaps' rectum. He knew PRECISELY the final impression he wanted to create in these cadets' minds. He slowly pivoted Ned around, so he now faced the class, using the collar and tie as a leash so the boys would SEE their teacher's red eyes and his flushed and tear-stained cheeks. Then, with a yank, he pulled Ned Belknaps to a standing position, pushing the buttocks slightly forward so that Ned appeared to be thrusting his abdomen TOWARDS those watching, at the same time CORKSCREWING his finger around and around the hapless man's anus.

The boys began to LAUGH! Nervously, raucously, with amusement or relief. What else could they do?

There, before them, was their pantless, spanked teacher, his crotch pushed toward them, and, from between his shirt-tails, his six-and-a half inch COCK—in FULL ERECTION! Due to The Commandant's unseen manipulations inside his ass, Ned's dick was HARD as FLINT! Wiggling his finger rapidly in Belknaps' rectum, Knighten made that STEELY pecker move, BOBBING RIDICULOUSLY up and down—POINTING this way, POINTING that. Mr. Knighten slowly turned his helpless victim to the right, then to the left, DISPLAYING Ned's PULSING PENIS from different angles for all the world to see.

For a full minute, The Commandant allowed the "viewing" to continue. The exhausted, STILL whimpering Belknaps could do nothing to alter his condition. He was COMPLETELY under the Marine's thumb, or better said, SLAVE to his finger! He was in a NIGHTMARE of UTTER EMBARRASSMENT from which he could not awake: BLUSHING, CRYING, PANTLESS, SOUNDLY SPANKED, and with all of this, sporting a HUGE HARD-ON! Only vaguely did he even register the echoing "HAR! HAR! HAR!" of wild laughter that reverberated off the walls of the classroom.

"Well, CADETS!" The Commandant shouted. He waited an instant to allow the laughing to subside. "It would appear that the MASTURBATING Mr. Belknaps has somehow actually ENJOYED his punishment before you!"

Commandant Knighten was in his element. He knew the cadets were his and his alone. They would not fool him. He knew it was likely their teenage cocks had been driven to the point of cumming at what they had witnessed. But he had dealt with MEN for long enough to know how slight the line was between amusement and desire. Now, he needed some FINAL act to truly SEAL his victory.

"Sergeant Pierce!"

Mr. Knighten's young assistant, mouth open in ASTONISHMENT before the scene he was witnessing, suddenly remembered himself and snapped to attention.

"Yes, Sir!"

"Retrieve Mr. Belknaps' underwear!"

"Yes, SIR!" Pierce scrambled to find Ned's boxers on the floor.

During the paddling, they had been accidentally kicked to the side, and variously stomped and stepped on as the punishing cadets had returned to their seats. The Sergeant held them up, wrinkled and covered with dusty footprints. At least, Pierce thought, perhaps The Commandant would allow his victim to cover himself now.

"Sir!" He handed the dirty underwear to Mr. Knighten.

"Very good, Pierce. Mr. Belknaps! Having now been made an EXAMPLE OF before these 30 cadets," The Commandant intoned, "You will NOW be an example BEFORE ALL OF BROWNSFIELD ACADEMY!" He wadded the shorts in his fist. "But FIRST, we must deal with your CHILDISH BLUBBERING!" He suddenly rammed his finger even deeper into Ned's asshole.

"AHHH!" Ned yelled.

As soon as he did, The Commandant STUFFED Ned's soiled underpants into his open mouth. He pushed them far back in his throat. Ned's cheeks BULGED like a squirrel's, and his red eyes popped open in SHOCK. The fly of his own shorts dribbled from between his lips. What a sight for the 30 cadets— their WELL-SPANKED, TEARY-EYED, SCARLET-RUMPED, FINGER-FUCKED instructor, there before them with a RAGING BONER, and EATING HIS OWN SHORTS!

This sight, of course, particularly the look of utter SURPRISE on Mr. Belknaps' face, led to another explosion of truly KNEE-SLAPPING mirth, exactly as the Commandant had anticipated.

Finally, twisting Ned's right arm behind his back and wiggling his finger roughly in Ned's rectum, Mr. Knighten pushed the hapless teacher toward the door. "Now, MARCH!!"

EXHAUSTED from SPANKING, his FANNY in flames, WEAK from CRYING, his legs like RUBBER, the Commandant's finger RAPING his rectum, the pantless, punished instructor could offer no resistance. The powerful ex-Marine in his resplendent uniform—hardly ruffled, it seemed, by all his exertion—propelled the punished, half-naked Ned from the classroom and out into the hall.

There, the vaunted discipline of Brownsfield Academy had disintegrated almost completely. The corridor was JAMMED not only with uniformed cadets, but with their instructors as well. Word of what was happening had spread like wildfire. The boys on guard duty had made sure of that. The Commandant caught Mr. Belknaps masturbating in the men's room! The Commandant dragged Mr. Belknaps down the hall with his pants down! The Commandant smacked Mr. Belknaps' BARE BUTT right there! The Commandant is thrashing Mr. Belknaps in front of his class with a pointer! The CLASS is PADDLING Mr. Belknaps with The Corrector! The Commandant is SPANKING Mr. Belknaps OVER HIS KNEE with The Facilitator! Mr. Belknaps is KICKING! Mr. Belknaps is CRYING! Mr. Belknaps is BEGGING!! His ass is pink... red... PURPLE!! Mr. Belknaps is getting AN OLD-FASHIONED, BARE BOTTOM SPANKING!!!

Ned's punishment had, needless to say, lasted long past

the end of hour. As cadets crowded the hallways on their way to their next class, merely OVERHEARING the BLISTERING in progress had drawn them toward the commotion. Through the high-ceilinged corridors, the CRACK of wood and palm on RUMP and Ned's increasingly hysterical YOWLS had, if anything, seemed louder as they echoed and re-echoed. More than a hundred young men now milled in the corridor, trading rumors, and, of course, many was the cock straining painfully against trousers as the sounds of BLAZING DISCIPLINE filled the air. As The Commandant SPANKED, boys jostled for positions at the door to actually SEE the UNPRECEDENTED SPECTACLE—a FULL GROWN MAN across Mr. Knighten's knee, WAILING and WIGGLING like a little boy, feet FLYING in the air, half-NAKED and getting his BUTT BURNED OFF! Even the briefest view filled them with fascination. How could this be happening! It was INCREDIBLE!

The teachers had done their best to maintain order, but they themselves were gripped with both curiosity, and FEAR! What could possibly have happened to create this situation!

And, too, if this could happen to Ned Belknaps, what about each and every one of them!

Two in particular—Mr. Slopes, the physics teacher, and Mr. Paine, from German—glanced nervously at one another. My God! Only two weeks before, the pair had reported to The Commandant for their "monthly reviews"—in the basement of the academy at 8:00 a.m. on Saturday. Neither had realized till then the other was among Mr. Knighten's "special cases," instructors whose lack of performance meant not a bad report or termination, but A GOOD HARD SPANKING! The Commandant had made it clear he would have fired both for their students' lack of improvement, but, in their cases, he had given them a choice— employing his own particular "methods of encouragement.".

So the slightly built, red-headed scientist had his pants pulled down to perform a LUSTY LAPDANCE across their boss's knee as The Facilitator did its work on his VERY bare bottom, while the larger and heavier German had lowered his trousers and underwear, bent across a bench, and presented his burly, beefy behind for BRUISING application of BOTH The Corrector and The Commandant's garrison belt. How that physicist's feet had FLUTTERED as Knighten BLISTERED his smooth and freckled fanny. With barely a tuft of hair around his anus and physically small as he was, he truly LOOKED like a little boy to his bigger colleague as he struggled FRUITLESSLY over Knighten's knee. Too, given how fair he was, his fanny almost immediately turned a STUNNING SCARLET as the hairbrush smacked and SMACKED!

Of course, Paine himself had no reason to feel cocky. All too soon, his own broad and well-furred bottom was itself dancing a desperate German JIG as Knighten made it clear with wood and leather that Paine himself, in his eyes, was no more than an OVERGROWN BRAT! And, indeed, that was surely what the language instructor FELT as wiggled his hairy hips with every blow and PLEADED and PROMISED to do better. Both men had cried REAL TEARS before The Commandant was done with their punishment, and had stood together afterwards, pants still down, dicks dangling, redfaced and redreared, as The Commandant read them the riot-act and made it clear that, if their performance did not improve, yet more INTENSE correction awaited them next month.

Thus, both knew first hand Mr. Knighten's COMMITMENT to TRADITIONAL CORPORAL PUNISHMENT. Still, neither could have ever conceived that THIS could happen.

Neither could BELIEVE the sight they took in..

There in the doorway, there before them and the boggle-eyed boys stood their colleague, wrist pinned to his back by The Commandant's firm grip, bare from waist to socks, his still erect penis poking out before him, his fiery buns quite apparent despite the partial covering of his shirt tail, his own underwear dribbling from his lips, his furiously blushing cheeks streaked with tears--the OBVIOUS recipient of a THOROUGH and RELENTLESS SPANKING!

Mr. Knighten drew back his arm.

"Forward, MARCH!"   SMACK!   The Commandant's massive paw landed loudly on Ned's SWOLLEN, BLISTERED, RAVAGED rear!

"MRFFPHHH!" Ned shrieked in protest, the sound muffled by the shorts stuffed in his mouth.

SMACK! "Two. Three. Four!"

SMACK! "Two. Three. Four!"

"MRFFPHHH!… MRFFPHHH!"

So, before the assembled multitude, Ned Belknaps MARCHED!   Boner BOUNCING, bottom BLAZING, the Commandant SPANKED the pantless teacher down the corridor. The boys from his class poured through the door to mingle with those milling outside, and all followed this amusing and UNHEARD OF parade down the hallway, the sharp report of the ex-Marine's meaty palm on the 35-year old's bare behind reverberating rhythmically off the old walls of Brownsfield Academy.

Ned's horror at his humiliation knew no bounds. How many men and boys were WITNESS to what was happening to him—100? 200? He could hear, as he was propelled helplessly along, their LAUGHTER, their HOOTS of derision and delight, even the occasional REMARK from one boy to another ("God, his ass is red as a stop sign!" "You should have seen him kick when The Commandant spanked him with the hairbrush!" "I can't believe his dick's hard!" "Man, he wiggled so bad when I whacked him with The Corrector." "The Facilitator really made him squirm!" "He was really beating off in the bathroom?" "He was crying like some little girl!" "We could see right up his butthole, he was squirming around so much!"). Every time Mr. Knighten's hand connected with his rear end, Ned's mind flashed on an image what he must have looked like over the past hour or so: his flying feet, his waggling rump, the grimacing, blubbing expression on his face! And now this, DISPLAYED before the entire school! Gagged though he was, Ned sniffled uncontrollably as The Commandant whacked him quicktime down the hall.

SMACK! "Two. Three. Four!"

SMACK! "Two. Three. Four!"

Mr. Knighten knew now how this little lesson was to end. They were headed for the office, specifically for the corner in the foyer where a radiator stood, and where, in a locked case, various trophies, pennets, and other mementos of the history of Brownsfield Academy were kept. There was ONE reminder of olden times that, The Commandant thought gleefully, would put a perfect and final period to the sentence he had imposed this now thoroughly PUNISHED miscreant.

They rounded the corner into the entryway.

SMACK! "Two. Three. Four!"

SMACK! "Two. Three. Four!"

"MRFFPHHH!"

"SMACK! SMACK! Halt!" The Commandant pulled Ned Belknaps to a stop, then bellowed, "Pierce!"

The young sergeant fought his way through the jostling crowd, each seemingly determined to get the best view. The place was pandemonium! He himself was simply speechless, not only at what he had seen, but at the idea that the disciplinarian that his commander was would contenance this kind of blatant unruliness. It seemed a weird betrayal of everything the institution stood for.

Yet, he was certainly not going to question orders at this point.

"Yes, Sir!" he barked.

"Pierce!" Knighten barked. "Do you see that steam pipe there above the radiator?"

"Yes, Sir."

"With Mr. Belknaps' tie, secure his wrists to the pipe."

"Yes, Sir."

Pierce went about his business. He could not ever LOOK in Ned Belknaps' eyes as he removed his "power tie" from his shirt. God, his rear was a RED as his neckwear! Part of it was sympathy (how well Pierce KNEW his Commandant's belief in the POWER of spanking), part of it was embarrassment (how COULD he look into the face of someone so TOTALLY and PUBLICALLY humiliated!), part of it was the fact that, despite all his reservations, Pierce's own dick was still HARD as STEEL at all he had seen.

He removed Ned's tie and, without any ado, wrapped it around his wrists—Commandant Knighten helping out, of course. Pierce then lashed the tails of the tie to the steampipe there on the wall, just slightly above Ned's head. Belknaps was now secured to the wall, his erect penis resting between two of the loops of the (thankfully!) cool radiator, his feet on the floor. In this position, he was bent at a slight angle, so his rear end protruded into the entryway. This, along with his arms being raised, caused his shirttail to ride up, so virtually all his flaming fanny was on view.

At that moment, Pierce caught his fellow employee's expression—terrified, furious, anxious, wanting. But he could do nothing. He dropped his eyes to the floor. He was following orders.

"Very well, cadets!" The Commandant intoned. "Now, we will begin the very FINAL phase of Mr. Belknaps' punishment. He has been THRASHED, PADDLED, and SPANKED—and SPANKED AGAIN for his misdeed. He has been EXPOSED to you all. NOW, he will be DISPLAYED as an EXAMPLE! Selwyn!"

"Yes, Sir!" the young man replied instantly.

"From my office, bring me a stapler, a piece of paper of legal size, the marker in the tray of my desk drawer, as well as the display case key that is hanging behind my desk. Do I make myself clear?"

"Yes, Sir!" the young man snapped smartly, torn between terror and excitement.

"Very well. Carry on!"

Selwyn skittered into the office as the members of Brownsfield Academy looked on. There was Ned Belknaps— UTTERLY under The Commandant's control—bent forward, bare rear poking from beneath his shirt, wrists tied to the steam pipe in the entry hall. The buzzing commentary continued as all waited for the last chapter to this AMAZING experience. Inevitably,

COCKS were still bursting against flies, but those observing did their best to control themselves. They were MILITARY "men," after all, and the PRICE of a lack of self-control was all too evident!

Knighten knew what he wanted from that cabinet. There within, saved from God-knew-when, was the DUNCE CAP that had been used when Brownsfield Academy was young—yellow, conical, a dark reminder of a serious past. And now, it would be planted on the HEAD of smart-ass teacher Belknaps.

Selwyn returned. Idly, Vasquez thought about how HE needed to be fucked—gangbanged actually, little wimp always doing what he was told! He imagined that Selwyn's swimmer's butt was still virginal, certainly tighter than Marksbury's well-drilled hole, and how he would bleat before the steady slamming of a thick Chicano blaster until finally Vazquez made him squeal with delight.

"SIR!" Selwyn stood with all the required implements in his arms.

"Very good, cadet." Knighten said softly.

He first leaned on the display case and, on the paper Selwyn had provided, carefully wrote 'MASTURBATOR' in bold print on the white, legal-sized sheet. Then, with the stapler, he folded Ned Belknaps' shirt halfway up his back, exposing that FIERY BEHIND completely, and affixed in place the page that identified the teacher's sin. He stepped back to admire his handiwork. Indeed, that BOTTOM was in FULL VIEW, and over it hung a sign that identified the misdeed that made Mr. Knighten, Commandant of Brownsfield Academy, do what he HAD to do.

Then, with Belknaps bound and gagged and now identified, he snapped the padlock on the display case and removed that yellow cap. He held it for a moment: almost two feet tall with the word "DUNCE" lettered neatly front and back, with two ties hanging on either side so it could be firmly anchored to the head. Those were the days! he thought. How many cadets had stood humiliatingly in the corner in the classroom or the hall with this hat upon their heads? Had they been paddled as well for their lack of effort? Were their pants around their ankles to expose their rosy rears? Inevitably though, he had to wonder if any former Commandant had EVER extracted a punishment so EXCRUCIATINGLY intense and appropriate as he had imposed on Ned Belknaps.

As he turned, something else caught his eye—a miniature baseball bat, about 8 inches long, with a faded red ribbon attached to it that read "STATE B-B FINALS/3rd/1933." It was a trophy from Brownsfield's pre-War past, when its baseball team had gone all the way to the State Championships. Knighten grinned. He had an inspiration! What would those boys, most of them probably gone to meet their Maker by now, think of how he now would employ the talisman of their victory. From now on, it would be a symbol of his OWN triumph!

He walked to Ned Belknaps' side. Without a word, he planted the conical cap atop the head of the bound and gagged instructor, and tied it FIRMLY in place. A hush had fallen over the entire crowd observing. There stood Ned Belknaps, 35 years olds, pantless and punished in his shoes, socks, and shirt. On his back was a sign identifying him as a masturbator, atop his head, a hat that marked him as a dunce, though, of course, for all, the SUREST marker of the Commandant's victory was Ned's BLISTERED, BATTERED, and very BARE BOTTOM, fully exposed to public view. Even somebody wandering in from the street would have no doubt that here, despite his age, was someone who had obviously suffered a LONG, HARD and HUMILIATING SPANKING!

The Commandant stepped back, and then, turning, retrieved the tiny trophy from the display case. He tapped it menacingly against his palm.

"Cadets," he said softly. "Today you have witnessed the kind of discipline that Brownsfield Academy imposed upon those—ALL those!—who violate its standards of self-control. I will not explain to you the precise methods of Mr. Belknaps' self-abuse. I will say only that it not ONLY involved parts of the body you might expect, but those many men are loath to touch. Still, I think YOU deserve to know, and that HE deserves a REMINDER of what I observed. Since he seems to have so ENJOYED being EXPOSED and SOUNDLY PUNISHED in the most JUVENILE fashion possible before you all, perhaps at least THIS will produce some MANLY SHAME in him!"

The Commandant waved the miniature baseball bat in front of Ned's face.

"OH MY GOD!" Ned thought. "He WOULDN'T!"

He was not alone in his stunned response. Sgt. Pierce could not believe it. Green and Steele put their hands to their mouths in ASTONISHED delight. Marxbury squirmed involuntarily, his butthole squeezing, knowing what was coming.

Knighten scanned the crowd of cadets, his eyes alighting on the two broadest and beefiest cadets in his view. "Arkanian! Vasquez!"

The massive shotputter and boxy wrestler snapped to attention.

"Pry Mr. Belknaps' legs apart and hold him that position!"

"YES, SIR!"

The two boys scrambled forward—Arkanian to the right, Vazquez to the left—and bent to do as they were commanded. Insodoing, both caught a POWERFUL and UNFORGETTABLE whiff of the unmistakable scent of SPANKED BOTTOM! It was a heady mix of sweat both rank and fresh, of asshole and hot skin. Poor Arkanian's cock began to spasm once again, and Vazquez's own dick poked painfully against his belly. Positioned as they were, they both got an EXTREME close-up view of Ned's BLAZING butt, his firm cheeks SWOLLEN and SALTED with BLISTERS, almost FUCSHIA in color, his buttcrack DAMP and SLIMY with perspiration, his BUTTHOLE pulsing deep within. Arkanian felt almost faint, and, weirdly, felt a wild desire that he, of course, repressed, to actually KISS that FIERY fanny!

Both yanked Ned's legs roughly wide apart. Bent slightly forward as he was, his pouty anus BLOOMED forth for all the world to see from between his SMOULDERING buns.

Deliberately, delicately, The Commandant leaned over.

With the thumb and middle finger of one hand, he spread the exposed pucker wider so the pink of the tight rumpring was fully displayed. Then—slowly, slowly—he began to insert the miniature ball bat, like some oversize thermometer, into Ned Belknaps' rectum.

"MRFFPHHH! MMRRRFFFPPHHHMMMRRRRRYYYYP PPHHH!!" Ned strained against his bonds and howled into the shorts stuffed in his mouth. Though the trophy was not THAT large, and Ned himself obviously sometimes stimulated his anus with a couple fingers while masturbating, this was something altogether LONGER and THICKER than anything that had ever entered his asshole before. His SORE and SWOLLEN buttlips and tight rumpring resisted the BLUNT, ROUNDED end of the bat as the Commandant FORCED it forward with constant, deliberate PRESSURE, but resistance was hopeless.

"POP!"

The wooden shaft SNAPPED through his spasming sphincter and began its journey up a male's most secret sanctum. The varnished probe SCRAPED the tender skin of his pucker, and his gutwalls began to retreat as the UNSTOPPABLE INVASION continued.

"MMRRRFFFPPHHHMMMRRRRRYYYYPPPHHHH!!"

The cadets watched with delight and fascination as the Commandant violated their instructor's helpless, blistered ass. Every so often, Mr. Knighten would pause and remove his hand, so all could see the wooden stick protruding from between Mr. Belknaps' spread and blazing buttcheeks like the stub of a bobtailed dog. Then he would begin his assault again—pulling the baton slightly out before pressing it further inside. From their vantage, Arkanian and Vazquez could plainly see Ned's rumpring tightly gripping the bat as it gradually absorbed the rod pushed past them.

"MMRRRFFFPPHHHMMMRRRRRYYYYPPPHHHH!!"

Ned wiggled his rear desperately, but to no avail. His flaming fanny shivered and shook as the bat BORED up his bottom. From time to time, Mr. Knighten would move the stick from side to side or roll it between his fingers as it advanced IMPLACABLY into Ned Belkaps' insides, touching him in places that had never been touched, thus causing, to Ned's horror, his prick to rise ever HIGHER and HARDER between his legs. As the probe went ever deeper, Ned's dick even begin to weep clear drops of pre-cum as his superior FUCKED his hole with this memento of a long-forgotten ball team.

Sergeant Pierce's eyes were FIXED on that squirming backside, that pucker that widened, then narrowed as the bat slid further into Ned. He knew The Commandant would not stop until the WHOLE of that 8 inches had disappeared into Ned Belknaps' ass. Observing the scene, he could not help, though he tried to, wondering what his OWN pulsing prong would feel like RAMMING up a male chute. Certainly, he was familiar with how a cunt cradled a man's poker, but, now, he was forced to consider how distinctive it might be to feel an asshole—especially a GUY'S asshole—caressing his own considerable slab of down-home manmeat as it porked the warm insides of a bright red butt.

"MMRRRFFFPPHHHMMMRRRRRYYYYPPPHHHH!! MMRRRFFFPPPPPHHHH!!"

With three quarters of the bat implanted in Ned's anus, Mr. Knighten suddenly began to pump it roughly in and out. The bat's broad tip tapped and poked against Ned's tender rectum. Now, indeed, he was getting REAMED up the rear as sure as if, instead of a sports trophy, a member of that long-lost 9 were slamming his aching DICK up those giving guts. Ned's own pecker squiggled the empty air UNCONTROLLABLY, dancing before him like a band conductor's baton gone MAD. Sticky spunk glistened on the tip of his penis and began to drip to the floor.

Then, in one sharp stab, the Commandant SLAMMED the remainder of the bat into Ned Belknaps' bottom, so only the red ribbon announcing Brownsfield Academy's 1933 victory remained in view--a TRIUMPHANT FLAG drooping from the teacher's anus.

"MMRRRFFFPPHHHYYYYPPPHHHH!!" Ned shrieked.

Mr. Knighten stepped back.

At the same instant, Ned's dick began SPUTTER shamelessly. The head of the bat was now lodged FORCEFULLY against his prostate, and, without his being able to control it, his cock cranked out GOB after GOB of thick, shimmering manjuice, SHOOTING in arcs through the air as Ned shuddered and shivered as he SHOT his load.

And then, even The Commandant could not help but LAUGH. The masturbator, forced to COME before the assembled cadets! He folded his arms across his broad chest as he heard the boys joining in his glee. The laughter rose to almost hysterical heights! There stood Ned Belknaps—a DUNCE cap on his head, hands BOUND to a steampipe, his SHORTS stuffed in his mouth, his SHIRT TAIL stapled up, on it affixed a SIGN that told the whole world of his sin!

And below? Two burly cadets spread wide the malfactor's legs, NUDE from socks to waist, exposing to all his BLISTERED, BLAZING, WELL-SPANKED BOTTOM, his buttcrack SPLAYED to expose his ACHING ASSHOLE, from it fluttering a ribbon RED as those rearcheeks, announcing this rump had been subdued and driven to surrender not only OUTSIDE, but INSIDE as well!

And, on the radiator, the wall, the floor, in specks and spots and little puddles, was Ned Belknaps' SPERM! A few small blobs had even landed on his CHEEKS and CHIN, where one now drooled WRETCHEDLY in a narrow thread toward his chest. Though nothing could be further from the truth, the shiny semen seemed a sign he had actually TAKEN PLEASURE in being STRIPPED, SPANKED, and SCREWED by Mr. Knighten and the hard-bodied cadets of Brownsfield Academy!

Ned's body began to shake with yet another series of sobs at this realization, though, of course, for those watching, it appeared merely the afterspasms of his orgasm, and, indeed, the slit of his hard dick continued to leak the last of his nutnectar so the head of it shimmered like the scepter of a monarch-- the KING of PAIN and SHAME!

Many were the cadet cocks that, at the sight, spattered forth GEYSERS of glimmering gyzm—some against underwear, some against pants' legs, some—who cared who saw!—from unzipped flies up to the sky and onto the backs of other uniforms or onto the ancient boards of Brownsfield Academy. Never had they known the sheer POWER that male-to-male DOMINATION and DISCIPLINE possessed. Though they did not know it, some of those who had witnessed this INCREDIBLE scene at Brownsfield Academy had already had their lives changed forever.

"Cadets!" Commandant Knighten barked. "Today you have observed the PUNISHMENT that Brownsfield Academy rightfully extracts from those that violate its rules! There is no tenet of order more significant than self-control! Mr. Belknaps was unable to fulfill this most important of charges imposed upon all those who serve here, and so was subject to a SOUND and JUST reminder of the cost of its violation. As I said before, for those who lack SELF-discipline, discipline must be IMPOSED!"

Knighten gazed out on the sea of bright, young faces. "As the conclusion of his PENANCE, and as an OBJECT LESSON to you all, Mr. Belknaps will remain DISPLAYED on this site and in his present condition until 17:00 hours this afternoon. Every time you pass this place, every time you observe him here, REMEMBER the TERRIBLE PRICE this institution extracts from those who ignore its rules and ridicule its traditions. RECALL the cost of a LACK of manly SELF-CONTROL! Steel! Greene!"

The two still grinning and stiff-cocked cadets snapped to attention.

"SIR!" they chorused.

"You will return to the site of Mr. Belknaps' punishment and retrieve The Corrector and the pointer I first employed to discipline him, along with The Facilitator. You will then return here and serve as—ahem—a Dishonor guard for Mr. Belknaps during the established time of his public exposure." The Commandant half-turned toward Ned. "Should he make ANY move to escape, should he attempt ANY in any way to alter his situation, you are to apply the pointer and The Corrector, BRISKLY and VIGOROUSLY, to his BARE BUTTOCKS! If I hear that sound, I will come from my office, after a decent interval, to oversee your efforts. Then, when you are done, I will AGAIN employ The Facilitator, placing Mr. Belknaps across my knee and SPANKING him EVEN MORE SOUNDLY on his BARE BOTTOM than I have SPANKED him heretofore!"

The two smiling football players skittered away instantly.

At this point, Knighten leaned menacingly toward Ned, so only those closest heard what followed.

"You are free, Mr. Belknaps, when your punishment is concluded," he whispered darkly, "to take any steps you choose. I would remind you, however, that the Chief of Police is my cousin, and the editor of the *Times and News* is an alumnus of Brownsfield Academy. Should you wish EVERY DETAIL of what has occurred here today to become public knowledge in this ENTIRE county and, indeed, the entire STATE, you may, of course, file a complaint. I wonder, though, if you WANT such humiliating information to reach a wider audience than it already has. When you are released, I would suggest that you make the necessary arrangements to leave this institution, and this community, as fast as your bandy legs will carry you!"

"Mission accomplished, SIR!"

Steel and Greene had returned, the paddle, hairbrush, and improvised cane in hand. The Commandant accepted The Facilitator as the boys took their positions on either side of the dunce-capped instructor.

"Very well, cadets! You shall now return to classes. DISMISSED!" Mr. Knighten roared.

Slowly, the crowd dispersed. Needless to say, the randy boys were desperately trying to figure out how soon they might find at least a second of privacy to relieve the AWFUL pressure that made their cocks ACHE! Even those who had already come, some multiple times, were once again randy. It seemed unlikely there had EVER, in the entire history of Brownsfield Academy, been the number of THROBBING BONERS at any

ONE time. If the cadets were all too aware of the PUNISHMENT that masturbating at school might bring down upon them, they were conscious as well that their bodily needs could no long be ignored. Boys' rooms and broom closests were certain to be STICKY with puddle upon pool of boiling male SPUNK before the day was through.

As Marxbury returned to class, he felt a hand pass lightly across the tight seat of his uniform pants. He turned. It was Chen!

"Boy," the once shy Asian boy grinned, "I'm glad I'm not you!"

Suddenly Marxbury's asshole began to itch maddeningly.

"I'm gonna fuck you SILLY tonight!" The freshman hissed menacingly.

Marxbury then noticed Kelly smiling broadly at him, Pastori made an obscene gesture at him, pumping his middle finger in and out of his fist. Vazquez grasped his own crotch, his thick dick blatantly outlined by his wet pantsleg, and winked.

What Chen had said was true, of course. Marxbury's barracks buddies would use him like an UTTER WHORE tonight. He could not even imagine the number of cocks he would have to SUCK, balls he would have to KISS, assholes he would have to LICK, and stiff DICKS that would POUND his poor pucker! There was little question that, during the "designated hour," he would be getting it from both ends from the very first second to the last. Jeez, to service all these horny hounds, he might find himself subject to the "double-teaming" some of the boys had sometimes threatened him with!

Marxbury shuddered, for what they meant had been lovingly described to him. It would be not merely "a swordfight in your fucking mouth, dude!"—a pair of cocks simultaneously plunging past his lips to gag him as he was forced to suck two guys at once—but a pulsing probe pressing the lips of his pouting pucker while another was already lodged DEEP in his rectum. He had often heard how his equally underendowed predecessor had often submitted to this treatment, and how, according to those who had done the porking, there was NO sensation more satisfying for a massive, manly fuckpole than that of a SECOND dick drubbing against it as they both reamed the tight, hot, and velvety ring of a fully stretched male rearhole.

Regardless, there was no doubt that, by the time they were done with him, Marxbury could be sure he'd have a tummyful of sperm, and semen dribbling down his thighs all the way to his spread knees. His face would be streaked with dark and greasy skidmarks from cracks too carelessly cleaned, and his body would be covered in cum. He'd have to shower for an hour to get the harsh perfume of gyzm off his skin and out of his hair, and use gallons of mouthwash to remove the taste of bleachy spunk and rank hole and pissy dick and sweaty balls from his tongue! He'd be picking pubes from between his teeth till the cows came home.

He didn't even want to THINK of the condition of his tender anus and RAMMED and RAVAGED rectum after the last poker had PLOWED his boyhole! If never before, his male's slimslit would be transformed into nothing but the TWITCHING TWAT of a TOTAL SLUT by the RAMPAGING REAMING-RODS of his dorm-mates. He would be the COMPLETE CUNT of the lust-crazed boarders of Brownsfield Academy.

Tonight, as "house pussy," he would SURELY do his duty. And MORE!

Looking for SOME kind of silver lining in the otherwise dark cloud, he glanced over his shoulder at Ned Belknaps' radiating rear. Well, he thought, at least I won't get SPANKED! That would make too much noise there in the barracks. Observing the BATTERED and VIOLATED backside of his one-time instructor, Marxbury took some small comfort in the fact that he would not be kicking and crying across the knees of dorm mates tonight like some naughty little girl. He sighed. Of course, who KNEW what ingenious and devilish ways his male masters might invent in order to do THAT to him, too!

For the next hour and a half, Ned Belknaps remained on display—his bare bottom BLAZING, an 8" miniature baseball bat

STUCK up his anus, his DICK and BALLS against the radiator, his UNDERPANTS in his mouth and a DUNCE cap on his head. Greene and Steel made SURE he made no move to alter his condition, occasionally stroking pointer and paddle across his swollen, rosy rear, frequently giggling, providing running commentary on his humiliation: "Who knew, Mr. Belknaps, what a bad little brat you were!" "Yeah, a real little brat! But, gee, teach, you sure are a big crybaby!" "Is The Commandant really your daddy?" "You sure can kick those legs, Mr. Belknaps." "And you've got a real cute little butt! Especially when it's red as a cherry!" "You sure love that big stick up your rearend, doncha!" "Man, just tell us when and we'll fuck you till you sing!" "But first we'll have to blister your naughty ass, you bad boy!" "Ass! You mean his badboy's BOTTOM!" "Yeah, teach, that's all you got, just a snotty little BOTTOM!" "I don't know about snotty, but it sure is HOT!" "And that's a hot little pussyhole, too." "NO KIDDING! Hey, for our next test, teach, maybe you'd like us to do a class gangbang for our project!" "Yeah, Mr. Belknaps, I bet you'd LOVE to take ALL our hard dicks up your sweet butthole, one right after one after another." "Whoever made you come with his dick up your ass would get an 'A'!" "I bet there'd be A LOT of perfect scores!" "Ya know, O'Neal's cock is even longer than that ball bat. Ten whole inches!" "Man, I bet that would make you squeal like a pig when he porked you!" "And Arakanian's pecker's as big around as my wrist." "That'd stretch those buttlips so wide they'd SCREAM!" "You'd be walking BOWLEGGED when we got done with you!"

To Ned's horror, his cock remained half-hard between the rungs of the radiator. The ballbat against his prostate kept his penis in a state of helpless excitation. The soft stroke of Greene and Steele's instruments across his ravaged rear would make his asshole grip the hard stick jammed up his rectum, causing it to poke roughly at a man's most sensitive spot of all. Though still dazed by what had happened to him, The Commandant's hissed threats still echoed in his head. Surely, he had every reason to bring a staggering lawsuit against Knighten and Brownsfield

Academy itself.

But that would mean publicity, LOTS of publicity! His name would be all over every newspaper in the state; on every news broadcast on the TV and radio. Family, friends, his neighbors, the doctor, the boxboy at the market and the mechanic at the gas station—they would all know the details of his HORRIBLE HUMILIATION, that he had been caught MASTURBATING, that he had been dragged WITH HIS PANTS DOWN the hall, SWATTED on the way by the Commandant's massive palm, that his NAKED BACKSIDE had been THRASHED with the pointer before his class, that his very STUDENTS had PADDLED him to TEARS, and then he had been TURNED OVER THE COMMANDANT'S KNEE in front of them and SPANKED on his BARE BOTTOM with HAIRBRUSH and HAND till he was KICKING and CRYING like a little boy! Everybody would know he had then been MARCHED down the hall to the tattoo of SMACKS on his buns with his SHORTS in his mouth and his REAR on DISPLAY, to be STOOD in the corner, crowned with a DUNCE cap, a sign on his back, and have his ASSHOLE violated by a long, thick, wooden bat before an audience of HORNY CADETS! And he had EJACULATED RIGHT BEFORE THEIR EYES!

People would gossip about him, laugh at him, point him out to others. Everywhere he went, they would make smart remarks or ask him questions or tease him. His situation was impossible!

His only solution was escape.

As soon as the final bell rang, various boys dashed off to their homes or the barracks, but many soon returned, cameras in hand. They needed EVIDENCE, for who would BELIEVE the spectacle they had witnessed! Steele and Green made no move to dissuade them as flashbulbs popped and videos whirred. Newman had a new digital camera he had just received for his birthday. Ned, of course, could not help but hear their gabbling commentary on all they had witnessed in the course of the day: "Nobody'll believe these pictures!" "I just hope I can get these developed!" "That's why I used the Polaroid." "My brothers are gonna bust a gut when I show 'em this tape!" "Hey, don't forget to bring it to the party after the game on Friday!" "I'm gonna show these shots to Sally this afternoon before I prong the shit out of her!" "The guys where I work are gonna piss their pants, they'll laugh so hard!" "Especially when they find out what that ribbon's attached to!" "Make sure you get a shot of his face with him eating his shorts!" "I'm posting them on the net." "Hey, I've got a penpal in Australia on-line. Let me know where you put them."

And so it went. Ned knew in the moment it was not merely his career at Brownsfield Academy that was over, not only his residence in this town. His dunce-capped HEAD, his stuffed MOUTH, his flushed, cum-spotted, and tearstrained FACE, not to mention his BARE, BLAZING, SPANKED, and VIOLATED 35 year old BOTTOM would be available by this evening for anybody in the WORLD to see with the click of a mouse! Men and women, boys and girls, yellow, brown, and black, and white, in California, Georgia, France, or China—ALL would not only KNOW the EXCRUCIATING EMBARRASSMENT he had endured, but be able to VIEW the results. He would be an INTERNATIONAL laughingstock, pictures of his BLISTERED FANNY exchanged from continent to continent as people giggled in shock and disbelief at how NED BELKNAPS had been PUBLICALLY SPANKED by his superior after getting caught JERKING OFF in the men's room!

Ned hung his head, defeated.

Snap-pop!

Another shutter clicked and flashbulb strobed.

At precisely 16:30 hours, Mr. Knighten emerged from his office. He smiled at the scene that greeted him. Steele, Green, and a dozen cadets with cameras braced to attention, amidst them, of course, the bound, redreared, dunce-capped, dildoed Mr. Belknaps. He simply stood for an instant, trying to imagine a final and appropriate coda for this day's events. In his head, like a film, he replayed in reverse order the last hours—the

VIOLATION of the instructor's anus, the MARCH down the hallway, the HAND spanking, the BRUSH blistering, the PUBLIC paddling, the THRASHING with the pointer, the PANTS-DOWN PARADE to the classroom, the private PENIS-PULLING in the men's room…

Then, it struck him.

Of course! There was ONE traditional rumproasting implement that had NOT yet been employed. Knighten recalled the hulking, hairy heine of Mr. Paine, the German teacher, squirming FRANTICALLY last weekend as he had welted that burly and—thanks to The Corrector--already BLAZING butt again and again with echoing strokes of his garrison belt. Paine was a big man, a noted singer in the Luthern church choir, but there bent over with his underpants down (with the sniffling scientist Mr. Slopes, rubbing his OWN recently reddened rear, victim of The Facilitator, looking on), the barrel-chested baritone had SQUEAKED and SQUALLED his own little high-pitched ARIA as the Commandant leathered his PLUMP and FULLY FURRED manmounds to a FURIOUS shade of scarlet. How Herr Paine had "yiked" and "yowled" as the Commandant had CROSSHATCHED his hinderparts with SLASH after SLASH of the SINGING strop! How he had PLEADED and promised to do BETTER as Mr. Knighten had taught him a true lesson in "Teutonic authority" on his broad behind, both BARE and BEARISH!   Only when Paine began to snivel and SOB did the Commandant desist in his DEVASTATING thrashing, ordering the brawny burgher to kneel, NOSE to the floor, and pull his own big buns WIDE apart to reveal his BLINKING BUTTHOLE for ten final stinging SNAPS of his boss's BRUTAL belt.

Further, the Commandant realized, what with these boys with cameras, here was a chance for a real record to be made of punishment actually in progress, AND a means to reward Steel and Greene, who had been his willing assistants during the dramatic display of DISCIPLINE from the very first.

He approached the captive teacher, and, gently at first, ran his hand across those still TOMATO RED buttocks. Properly swollen. HOT to his touch. There was no question this rump would bear the evidence of its suffering for days if not WEEKS! Idly, he allowed his fingers to wander down Ned's SWEATY buttcrack, and tapped on the end of the ball bat, still lodged FIRMLY in his rectum. He then softly massaged the teacher's RACKED posterior, enjoying how Belkaps squirmed and moaned at his touch. He began to rub more ROUGHLY, then PINCHED the rosy flesh—lightly at first, then HARDER! He grabbed a handful of ass and TWISTED it, then another and another. Suddenly, he pulled back his arm and administered a sharp POP to his employee's blistered bottom!

"Mmmppphhhffff!" Ned groaned.

"Gentlemen!" The Commandant announced to the cadets around him. "I believe Mr. Belknaps' backside has actually BEGUN to return to normal. But his punishment has not YET concluded! Perhaps it would be wise to give him one FURTHER dose of the DISCIPLINE we here at Brownsfield Academy extract before we send him on his way, a LAST reminder of his violation of our proud traditions." He paused. "Steel! Greene!"

"Yes, SIR!" the two football players answered smartly.

"REMOVE YOUR BELTS!"

The two boys looked at one another delightedly. Oh, WOW! It took little imagination to figure out what Mr. Knighten had in mind, and, by ordering them both to take off their belts, it was APPARENT what was in store. To administer a good WHIPPING, the Commandant himself would need only a single strap. The two cadets realized that THEY were to be the executioners of the FINAL PUNISHMENT of Ned Belknaps!

With terrific haste, the two unbuckled and slipped the leather bands—THICK and WIDE---from their pantsloops with a whispering "sshhhhh!" Without even being told, they doubled them over and stood at attention on either side of their incapacitated teacher, strops gripped TIGHTLY in their hands.

The Commandant grinned. "I see the two of you have ANTICIPATED your next order!" He placed his hands on his hips, and turned to face the other cadets. "Very well. Mr. Belknaps will now endure the indignity of a good FLOGGING on his BARE BUTTOCKS! Appropriately enough, this punishment will be undertaken by two fine examples of Academy MANHOOD, Mr. Steel and Mr. Greene. In order for this event to be duly and properly recalled, I encourage those observing to employ those means they have at hand to provide a RECORD of it. Cadets, aim your CAMERAS!"

He then returned his gaze to the two stars of the grid-iron. "Mr. Steel and Mr. Greene, at my signal, you will commence the WHIPPING of Mr. Belknaps' BARE BOTTOM—as always, BRISKLY and VIGOROUSLY! You will not cease until so ordered. Do I make myself clear?"

"Yes, SIR!" the boys shouted in unison.

"Very good!" The Commandant raised his arm. "Gentlemen…" His arm fell. "Commence THRASHING!"

CRACK!

Steel's belt SLAPPED across Ned Belknaps' rear with the report of a pistol shot.

CRACK!

Greene's strap lashed it almost INSTANTANEOUSLY afterwards.

CRACK! CRACK! CRACK! CRACK!

"MMRRRFFFPPHHHMMMRRRRRYYYYPPPHHHH!!" their teacher shrieked into his shorts.

Like LIGHTENING, the SLASHING strokes of the muscular youths BLASTED across Ned Belknaps' already PULVERIZED posterior! How COULD a pair of rumpcheeks sustain even MORE abuse, especially when delivered with all the power of these RIPPLING and ATHLETIC biceps? Ned's head jerked back, then forward, the yellow DUNCE cap SLICING through the empty air. His half-erect dick and balls were momentarily CRUSHED against the cold steel of the radiator, and then he began a DELIRIOUS DANCE, hopping foot-to-foot in a TOTTERING TWO-STEP as those boys' belts bore down again and again on his WEAVING and WAGGING behind.

CRACK! CRACK! CRACK! CRACK!

"MMRRRFFFPPHHHMMMRRRRRYYYYPPPHHHH! MRRRFFFPPHHH!! MMMRRRRRYYYYPPPHHHH!!"

Ned's muffled WAILS accompanied the BLISTERING bolts unleashed by Steele and Green. Their straps arced through space and connected UNFAILINGLY with the already SEARED seat of Belknaps' body, his FIERY FUNDAMENT put once again to the FLAME! Like young and proud Greek gods, the JEERING JOCKS sent SCORCHING stripes of rawhide WRATH across their instructor's BOUNCING behind! Filled with amusement and adreneline, Toby and Mike set about their task with UNBRIDLED enthusiasm, POTENT in their power and DETERMINED to show the Commandant his confidence in their capacity as MEN WHO SPANK! was not misplaced.

Their cocks, of course, TICKLED TERRIBLY, engorged and drooling, each STRIKE on rear the source of almost ELECTRIC pleasure in their balls as they swung each time with new ENERGY and ENJOYMENT. Throughout Ned Belknaps' ordeal, they had DREAMED, the two of them, of administering his punishment themselves, and, now, it was THEY who were IN COMMAND, the confident conquerors of this BARE and BUCKING breech! It was Mike Green and Toby Steele who composed the WHISTLING, CRASHING melody with belt and fanny to which their teacher performed a PATHETIC and PRANCING tarantella of PAIN!

CRACK! CRACK!
"MMRRRFFFPPHHHMMMRRRRRYYYYPPPHHHH!"
CRACK! CRACK!

Before the Commandant's amused eyes, Ned's punishment continued. He had surely chosen right in putting Steele and Green to the job of SPANKING THE REAR OFF this wretched jerkoff. There was absolutely no question the pair were giving their all to producing MAXIMUM punch to their every swipe at that WRIGGLING RUMP. Red as it was, Belknaps' backend now showed the unmistakable WELTS that only result from a SOUND STRAPPING!

CRACK! CRACK! CRACK!

"M M R R R F F F P P H H H M M M R R R R R Y Y !
MMRRRFFFPPHH!!"

Meanwhile, of course, again to Knighten's utter approbation, the remaining cadets were jostling one another MADLY to get the best angle, the most perfect perspective, on the PUNISHMENT in progress. Newman lay on the floor to get a shot from beneath as one belt exploded against Ned's WRITHING rear, while Lansdowne circled with his whirring video camera to capture the expression on his face and his erect member and JIGGLING nuts as well as his BUCKING bottom. Kelly popped another cartridge into his Polaroid, snapping picture after picture and allowing them to fall to the floor to be collected later as he strove to capture even instant of the THUNDERING thrashing!

CRACK! CRACK! CRACK! CRACK!

"MMRRRFFFPPHHHMMMRRRRRYYYYPPPHHHH!"

CRACK! CRACK!

Ned's rump was raw, pulsing, pounded PURPLE! He struggled CRAZILY to somehow escape the STINGING STRAPS that SEARED his bottom, but Sergeant Pierce—always the good soldier—had indeed tied the captive teacher so skillfully to the steampipe that his very attempts to escape actually TIGHTENED his bonds. The cowhide crisscrossing his already BATTERED buttocks sent shivers and shakes SHOOTING through all of Ned's nerves. In his JUMPING and JERKING, he appeared nothing so much as COMICAL CHARACTER in some semi-silent film played as FAST FORWARD—the sound effects the SHRIEKS and SNIVELS from his SHORT-STUFFED mouth and, of course, the virtually unbroken SNAP of STROP on SKIN produced by the SPANKING FURY of the team of Steele and Green!

CRACK! CRACK! CRACK!

"MMRRRFFFPPHHHMMMRRRRRYY!!"

The contemporary gridiron duo were, of course, not the only muscular examples of Brownsfield Academy's athletic glory engaged in the punishment of Ned Belknaps, at least in spirit. Deep inside the hapless instructor, the ghosts of ANOTHER group of Brownsfield boys extracted their own revenge upon moaning masturbator. As Ned's FRENETIC footwork and bouncing and squirming grew ever more FRANTIC, that team trophy of 1933 RAVISHED his rear as surely as if he had been transported through time and tied BAREASS across a BENCH so those champions of the diamond might TAKE THEIR PLEASURE with their COCKY cranks up his tight maletwat, one after another. That 8" ballbat moved every which way in Ned Belknaps' ROILING rectum--BANGING its walls, POKING his prostate, PROBING that posterior in ways unimaginable, the red ribbon fluttering from his anus like a FLAG!

CRACK! CRACK! CRACK! CRACK!

"M M R R R F F F P P H H H M M M R R R R R Y Y! MMRRRFFFPPHHHHHHHH!!"

Though Ned could not know it, nor the Commandant, nor Steele, nor Green, nor those whose cameras immortalized this particular event in the long history of Brownsfield Academy, those cadets of '33 would probably have SMILED to know how the symbol of their prowess had ultimately been employed. Of course, a rosy rump, for them, would have no particular reason for comment. Their fannies were surely no strangers to BARE BOTTOM DISCIPLINE! Indeed, in THEIR day, boys did not enjoy the privilege of privacy when punishment was due. Their pants-down paddlings did not proceed in the Commandant's office, but rather RIGHT ON THE SPOT—in the classroom, the hallway, the athletic field. Teacher or Coach, it mattered not--all had the option of exposing a cadet's BLUSHING BACKSIDE to FULL PUBLIC VIEW in order to administer a SOUND SPANKING with his implement of choice.

There was, for example, not one single member of that long-lost team—first baseman, right fielder, shortstop, batboy, or manager--who had not found himself, not ONCE but MANY TIMES, grabbing his ankles in chemistry or turned across a desk in English or sprawled across a man's lap in history (taught by the well-known BLISTERER, Mr. Thomas), trousers to his ankles and skivvies to his knees, wiggling his PERT POSTERIOR at his peers as palm, paddle, strap, ruler, cane, and, yes, even a hairbrush or two extracted the PAINFUL PRICE for the miscreant's misdeed.

In fact, the forgotten baseball coach of that era—Abner Oglethorpe by name, a towering Texan with arms corded with muscle —was FAMOUS for PULLING HIS PLAYERS' PANTS DOWN at practice or even at a GAME or two and hauling them OVER HIS KNEE when their performance was not up to par! FEW could forget the sight of the unfortunate senior center fielder—Hillman, by name--who, after a botched catch in the eighth inning of a close game, found himself FLIPPED ACROSS Oglethorpe's leg, knickers AND drawers at half-staff, CREAMY buns facing the crowd, nor the SOUND of the Coach's HARD HAND as he SMACKED that player's BARE and BUCKING behind to a SULTRY shade of crimson one humid afternoon. Literally HUNDREDS—his team mates, the other team, the officials, and all the fans (men and women, boys and girls)--had watched as the hulking Hillman—usually a star player—was reduced to a BAWLING BRAT across his coach's knee that day, that CALLUSED palm and WRIGGLING rump giving new meaning to the word "error!" The hapless boy was known ever after, particularly among the German population in town, as "HOT HEINIE HILLMAN."

Perhaps knowledge of THAT incident might have given Ned Belknaps some comfort.

Still, rather than his palm, Oglethorpe generally favored a four inch wide FENCE SLAT—polished smooth by ENDLESS encounters with BARE CADET BUNS—as the best means to instill TRUE discipline in the young men under his tutelage. A loss on the ballfield, every player knew, meant a DETOUR on the way to the showers, a detour across the phonepole thighs of Mr. Oglethorpe, seated in the alcove, fence slat in hand!

And NONE were excused! The failure was the TEAM'S, and so each members' TAIL must PAY the price. Naked feet FLEW and naked butts BURNED and naked boys CRIED as they learned the cost of one of their numbers crummy fielding, a muffed at bat, or any other missed opportunity. If a loss on the field was ESPECIALLY embarrassing or egregious, the Coach remained at his station at the shower room door so that not only was each behind WELL-BURNISHED on the way to wash up, but on the way BACK—when those now MOIST and already TENDER malemounds were subjected to yet ANOTHER and more SEVERE slapping with Oglethorpe's spanking slat!

"MMRRRFFFPPHHH! MMMMMMRRRFFFPPHHH!"

CRACK! CRACK! CRACK! CRACK!

But the class of '33 had yet another claim to fame, inherent in its very name. No one knows who first noticed it, but that number itself was the source of GREAT teasing and amusement to those of other classes at Brownsfield Academy. If '69' seemed to show two people—male or female--engaged in mutual pleasure, '33' seemed to imply even more vividly a different sexual act—the first 3 was the buttocks of a SUBMISSIVE cadet, spread and presented to the second 3, the dominant cadet who had MOUNTED him. The two together, the 33, OBVIOUSLY showed a DEEP buttfucking very much in process!

And so, the Class of '33 (unofficially, of course) had been known among their fellow cadets as "THE ASSCRAMMERS"—a name not entirely inappropriate. Perhaps it was to live up to their reputation, but the youths of '33 were, for many years, known as the most NOTORIOUS buggers in the history of Brownsfield Academy. The boarders had their "house pussy," but it was well-known that, during the "designated hour," if the line were too long for a horny boy to wait, he might negotiate, from many of his fellows in any case, a little SPONTANEOUS pleasure with two flips of a coin. The process was simple. The first flip determined the position of each cadet—heads for the "guy" and tails for the "gal." The second, of course, then determined WHAT mode of enjoyment the "guy" would experience: "heads" for his "gal's" SOFT, WET mouth; "tails" for his TAUT, TIGHT rectum. On certain nights, the story went, there was not a boarding cadet in the barracks who, between 4:00 and 5:00 in the morning, was not either FUCKING or GETTING FUCKED.

CRACK! CRACK! CRACK!

"MMRRRFFFPPHHH! MMMMMMRRRFFFPPHHH!"
CRACK! CRACK! CRACK! CRACK!

There were in those of '33 certain boys who even seemed to LIKE to service their classmate's cocks. The captain of the hockey team—a broad shouldered boy named "Ames"—was whispered to have taken SIX of his teammates dicks up his freckled rear one after another, and then have shoved the BLADE of a HOCKEY STICK up his asshole and jerked himself off to their collective applause!

And it was not just the boarders who were notorious. A group of day students known as "THE DICKDRUBBERS" were said to gather every Saturday night after their dates at the malt-shop or the Rialto, there to STRIP NAKED and drink and DIDDLE their DANGLING DONGS as well as their ASSHOLES in circle jerks that lasted for HOURS! Another, even more secretive clan, which included FIVE members of that very baseball team, called themselves "THE RAMS," and got together for sessions of, unsurprisingly, "poker" and beer. In those Depression days, of course, no money was placed on the table, but rather articles of clothing, and when FINALLY one of their number lost his underpants and stood BUCKNAKED before the others, he was required to offer up BOTH his TONGUE and REAR for whatever pleasure the winners demanded. Ironically, it was the PITCHER, not the catcher, of Brownsfield's baseball team who was rumored to often LOSE ON PURPOSE, so his fellow Rams might employ his mouth AND ass in any way they saw FIT!

"MMRRRFFFPPHHH! MMMMMMRRRFFFPPHHH!"
CRACK! CRACK! CRACK! CRACK!

So it was, perhaps, only APPROPRIATE that the symbol of victory of the Class of '33 was now MERCILESSLY plowing Ned Belknaps' bottom! Given his DESPERATE dancing and squirming, that ballbat set on a true RAMPAGE to ever corner of his RIPE and VIRGIN RECTUM. And yet—ironically—despite the BURNING swipes across his already BLISTERED buns by the belts of Steele and Green, despite the knowledge his NAKED REAR was being PUBLICALLY WHIPPED by two boys more than 15 years his junior, despite the fact that he was in a haze of EMBARRASSMENT and his BROILING BUNS were in AGONY, Ned nonetheless retained a partial ERECTION as his ass was STRAPPED and SCREWED. Like some giant switzle-stick, the bat STIRRED his guts into a FRENZY of never-known pain-pleasure. His occasional anal play when he beat off had simply not prepared him for the ELECTRIC chills that passed through him as that HARD, THICK stick EMBEDDED in his butthole POLED and PROBED the most PRIVATE part of his anatomy. Through the BURN of the flogging by the two MIGHTY cadets, some small part of Ned's brain understood, in a flash, how it was that since the very beginning of time males might BEND OVER, SPREAD THEIR RUMPCHEEKS WIDE and BEG another MALE to use his LONG, THICK, and THROBBING DICK to give him a GOOD, LONG, HARD FUCK UP THE ASS!

And at that realization, his penis poked up yet ANOTHER notch!

It was not, of course, only the TEACHER'S pecker that was tingling. Those taking picture all had BULGING boners, while, for Steele and Green, it was as if there were a WIRE which delivered a direct power connection from their SINGING STRAPS through their shoulders and chests and stomachs down to their crotches and on to the VERY TIPS of their FROTHING and FLINTY DICKS! Sweat SOAKED their armpits and DRIPPED from the foreheads, but STILL they SPANKED, their belts a BLUR, that BOTTOM the target of all their lusty, youthful energy. NEVER had either enjoyed such PULSING POTENCY, such a sense of ABSOLUTE DOMINANCE, never had their balls BOILED with such SEETHING sexuality, nor their reamers BURST with such ROILING RANDINESS as in these moments they leathered the DANCING DOMES of their teacher's TWITCHING tail.

CRACK! CRACK! CRACK! CRACK! CRACK!

"MMRRRFFFPPHHH! MMMMMMRRRFFFPPHHH!!!"

The Commandant glanced at his watch. He was enjoying the scene spread out before him tremendously. What specimens of Brownsfield Academy MANHOOD were Steele and Green,

CERTAINLY cadets after his own heart. How THOROUGHLY they BLISTERED those bucking buttocks! How TIRELESS they were in their disciplinary task! How COMPLETELY they seemed to understand the SINGULAR sensation of administering a GOOD, HARD SPANKING!

And Ned Belknaps! Now THERE was someone who had been taught a lesson he would NEVER forget! How effectively, Knighten thought, he himself had carried to its conclusion his campaign of ABSOLUTE HUMILIATION. His SCORCHED RUMP policy had, here, reached its apogee. He doubted, in the history of Brownsfield Academy, had any rear been PUT TO THE TORCH more FURIOUSLY, nor had anyone witnessed such ABJECT and UTTER surrender to the PAINFUL POWER of an old-fashioned BARE BOTTOM BLISTERING!

CRACK! CRACK! CRACK! CRACK! CRACK!

"MMRRFFPPHH! MMMRRFFPPHH! MMRRRFFPPHH!!!"

CRACK! CRACK! CRACK! CRACK!

He sighed. Still, all good things must end. He had left Sergeant Pierce his orders, and the appointed time for the conclusion of the smart aleck Mr. Belknaps' punishment was drawing nigh.

Reluctantly, he drew in a deep breath.

"CADETS!" he bellowed. "CEASE SPANKING!!"

CRACK! CRACK!

Green and Steele—slowly; indeed, GRUDGINGLY-- dropped their arms. For an few instants, the afterglow of their final strokes kept Ned Belknaps dancing, and his muffled YOWLS continued.

"MMRRRFFFPPHHH! MMMMMMRRRPPHHH!"

Then, a strange silence settled through the halls of the Academy, broken only by the winded breathing of the two athletic cadets, and Ned's own stopped moaning.

"Gentlemen," The Commandant intoned, "you have done your duty and done it well. You are a credit to Brownsfield Academy, AND to notions of SOUND and TRADITIONAL discipline! I am certain Mr. Belknaps will LONG remember the

LESSON you have taught him!"

The two football players BEAMED. What a WORKOUT! Steele thought, smiling. It was too bad his teacher's ass was not available on a DAILY basis in the gym! This was a HELL of a lot more fun than lifting weights!

Green, meanwhile, had his hands on his knees, catching his breath, though that was not the ONLY reason he bent forward. His hard twat-thwacker was absolutely SCREAMING, weeping copious amounts of pre-cum all over his crotch. He DESPERATELY needed RELEASE!

The smiling Commandant could not resist one final touch. He reached in his pants pocket, and pulled out a thick-tipped marker. Thank God its ink was BLACK. At this point, given the condition of the butt before him, RED would surely not do! SWOLLEN, BLISTERED, BRUISED,WELTED and WEALED, Ned Belknaps' bottom was a brilliant, angry SCARLET—a deep wine color almost PURPLE!

Knighten took a good look. He recalled a symbol he had seen once that well encapsulated the condition of the instructor's rear:

(#!#)

Then, without further ado, he stepped forward, and on Ned Belknaps battered behind, he neatly wrote two words just below the crest of each bun—one on one cheek, one on the other:

(~~BAD!BOY~~)

He stepped back. He could imagine the trouble the sassy Mr. Belknaps would have REMOVING the little message now INSCRIBED on his buttocks! The ink of the pen was of the "indelible" variety. It could, of course, with sufficient soap and scrubbing, be lifted from the skin, but, surely, it would be DAYS before the teacher could stand anything but the most TENTATIVE touch to his well-burnished behind, MUCH LESS the PRICKLING BRISTLES of a BRUSH that would speed the process along. But the use of any brush, of course, would have to bring to mind, for Ned, the SPECTACLE he had made of himself as he FLOPPED and FLAILED across the Commandant's KNEE as he was getting SPANKED!

Further, the Commandant knew well enough that, inevitably, Ned would be inspecting his fanny on a regular basis—not just in the morning, but several times a day, maybe hour to hour!—in the hopes that the evidence of his rump's ordeal had passed away. He smiled as he imagined the frustration of this fuck-up, drawers and trousers down, standing before the mirror, his head twisted around—not just this week but probably the next and possibly the next as well—confronting his still RUDDY rear and those only faintly faded words that PROCLAIMED his shame!

Thirty-five years old, but still NOTHING but a "BAD BOY" among MEN!

Knighten turned, exhaled, and, with a certain sadness, addressed the cadets for the penultimate time that day: "Snap your final pictures, men!" he barked.

Those assembled were only to happy to oblige, LAUGHINGLY obeying their Commandant's command. There was a momentary blaze of flashbulbs and strobes, the click of shutters and whir of the video camera.

The Commandant then continued: "At 17:00 hours sharp, Mr. Belknaps, Sergeant Pierce will retrieve your trousers from your classroom, then release you. He has orders to then leave you with the privacy to clothe and compose yourself.

"SHOULD you decide to continue with your appointment at Brownsfield Academy, I will expect you to report tomorrow morning at PRECISELY 07:23 hours to your classroom. Needless to say, given your conduct, I will be WAITING there, and I will be PERSONALLY supervising your teaching throughout the day. I will be accompanied by Cadet Steele and Cadet

Green. And I WARN you, I will have what I believe was, FOR YOU, today's most EFFECTIVE disciplinary instrument—THE FACILITATOR—close at hand!

"Should you be even ONE minute late, I—PERSONALLY and IMMEDIATELY—will proceed to STRIP YOU COMPLETELY NAKED and STAND YOU IN THE CORNER! I can ASSURE you that you will be placed so as to be in FULL VIEW of those passing by the open door, so ALL will be aware of your PENDING PUNISHMENT! Should anyone—faculty or cadet--enter the room to INSPECT you more closely in your HUMILIATED STATE, I will make NO move to impede them. Indeed, should they wish to determine the condition of your buttocks—to feel, fondle, or to STRIKE them with the open hand—I will ENCOURAGE them to do so!

"At the 08:00 bell, when your class is assembled (which, as I recall, is one of your sections of freshman world history) I will guide you BY THE EAR to the FRONT of the classroom, where--IN THE BUFF, of course--you will NEATLY write 'I WILL NOT BE LATE TO WORK.' on the central quadrant of the blackboard--100 times, left to right, and numbered. I will be standing by with the pointer, and should I feel you are being slow or sloppy in completing your assignment, I will IMMEDIATELY administer FIVE strokes of the pointer—BRISKLY and VIGOROUSLY—across your BARE BACKSIDE to encourage you to do better.

"When you have completed your task, I will then again TAKE YOU BY THE EAR and PUT YOU over my knee BEFORE THE CLASS. In that position, you will be SOUNDLY lectured regarding your misdeed, your posterior facing outward so the young men may have a GOOD look at you in your CHILDISH circumstance. I suspect a good FIVE MINUTES of talking to will be necessary to impress upon you the significance we place upon BEING ON TIME here at Brownsfield Academy.

"After that, Mr. Belknaps, I will proceed, as you might guess, to administer a GOOD, HARD SPANKING on your BARE BOTTOM with the HAIRBRUSH until you are CRYING YOUR EYES OUT!

"After that, I will STAND before your students and you will APOLOGIZE to them for your tardiness.

"From that point on, you will be required to conduct NOT ONLY that class but ALL your classes IN THE NUDE, so that your private parts AND your RED and UNRULY RUMP are on PUBLIC DISPLAY to your students as a reminder to all of the VIRTUE of PUNCTUALITY! I am certain the cadet corps will be QUITE amused at your condition, Mr. Belknaps, but THAT is YOUR problem, NOT mine. I suspect, each time you turn to the blackboard and so expose your BLISTERED BUTTOCKS to their eyes (and I can ASSURE you they WILL be BLISTERED!), there will be a certain amount of comment and giggling. THAT you will simply have to deal with!

"Further, you may be SURE I will remove the lectern from the room and ask Cadets Steele and Green to move your desk to the wall, so you will NOT be able to hide behind them while teaching. Hence, either your posterior or your testicles and your penis—hard or soft, it matters not--will be IN FULL VIEW of ALL present at ALL times." The Commandant chuckled. "Of course, from your performance before us today, it appears you may actually PREFER to teach your classes in such an exposed state."

Knighten's face hardened once again. "Regardless, you will be expected to maintain an ORDERLY classroom. Should the students become unruly, I will look upon that as YOUR responsibility, and you will IMMEDIATELY be PLACED ACROSS MY KNEE again for an even more SEVERE SESSION with The Facilitator!

"To RE-ENFORCE this lesson for as many members of the Brownsfield community as possible, your written lines will REMAIN on the blackboard, and, at the beginning of EVERY hour subsequent, before you begin the day's lesson, you will apologize for your tardiness and receive yet ANOTHER GOOD, HARD SPANKING on your NAKED FANNY! In that applying SIX such spankings may test even MY stamina, I will determine, class to class, whether I will administer your discipline, or if I will designate Mr. Greene, Mr. Steele, or one of the CADETS

ENROLLED IN THE CLASS to take you across HIS lap to APPLY TO HAIRBRUSH to your exposed behind!

"But make no mistake, Mr. Belknaps, ALL spankings you receive, whether conducted by me, Green, Steele, or one of your students, will continue until you are KICKING YOUR FEET IN THE AIR and you are IN TEARS, no matter how long it takes! I believe," he added dryly, "you yourself are perfectly aware that these fine MEN—even the youngest--are as FULLY CAPABLE as I am of administering a spanking BRISKLY AND VIGOROUSLY, and MAKING YOU KICK AND CRY with great GUSTO!

"During lunch hour, you will be MARCHED down the hall--ALWAYS IN THE NUDE—to STAND beside my office. As occurred today, count 'one' will consist of a sound SMACK to your buttocks, though, rather than my hand, I will employ The Facilitator to administer your well-deserved swats! You will then be placed beside my door with your NOSE to the WALL as a sign of the DISHONOR you have brought upon Brownsfield Academy. As has occurred today, members of the cadet corps will be allowed, indeed, ENCOURAGED, to observe, comment on, and RECORD your humiliating circumstance as they see fit. As you are aware, all visitors to the Academy must first sign in with Sergeant Pierce, so they too, of course, will be witness to your circumstances. I can think of three deliveries due tomorrow in addition to the mail, so you may be sure that word of your condition will NOT be restricted to the confines of this institution!

"Subsequently, I will MARCH you back to your room for your afternoon classes, when there will be NO alteration of this regimen of PUBLIC NAKEDNESS, of APOLOGY and SOUND, OVER-THE-KNEE SPANKINGS on your BARE BOTTOM! I intend to be CERTAIN you have learned your lesson and will demonstrate, in the future, proper RESPECT for the rules and traditions of Brownsfield Academy."

The Commandant then had an inspiration. "As I remember, Mr. Belknaps, during sixth period, which begins as 14:05 hours, you are normally free, in that it is your 'prep' time, during which you plan for the next day before your seventh hour class.

It also happens to be the time that both the water polo and gymnastic teams are convened in the gymnasium for practice. At the two o'clock break, you will once again be MARCHED THROUGH THE HALLS in the same fashion as before, this time to the gym. There, I will sit you in a chair, which I suspect will be MORE than a little uncomfortable for you. I will then ask Coach Standback to retrieve the implements employed by the water polo team to improve their speed and performance in the water. I refer, of course, to the clippers and safety razors.

He smiled. "To begin, I will first give you a PROPER HAIRCUT—a Number 1 buzz that, as I assume you know, is standard for a recruit in the Marine Corps, and should serve as a reminder to you that this IS, in fact, a MILITARY institution dedicated to DUTY, DISCIPLINE, and SELF-CONTROL!

"That will NOT, however, be the end of things, Mr. Belknaps. I believe that all who have witnessed your punishment today—indeed, even YOU—would agree that your response has been NOT that of a grown man, but a MERE BOY! Your conduct, from the moment I encountered you in the act of self-abuse in the faculty men's room, has been that not of an adult, not even an adolescent, but of a small child. Given that this is the way you ACT, so it should be the way you APPEAR!

"Hence, I will invite the gymnastics team to secure you to the vaulting horse—first, face up. Then, in such fashion as they choose, they will remove not ONLY your moustache, but any other MANLY HAIR elsewhere on your body below the eyebrows—your chest, your belly, your legs, and most especially, of course, from your crotch, from elsewhere around your penis, and from your testicles.

"At that point, the water polo team will be invited to take over. They will TURN YOU OVER and secure you FACE DOWN over the horse, and will be invited to shave your legs and your backside, INCLUDING, of course, the area between your legs, between your buttocks, and around your anus. After your spankings, I would suggest, your bottom in particular will be VERY tender as it is spread for the team to do a complete and thorough a job as possible. As with all else, however, such discomfort on your part is not MY concern!

"When this task is done and you have been COMPLETELY denuded of ALL hair, I will send Mr. Steele to my office to retrieve The Corrector. Then, as occurred today in your class, the gymnastics team AND the water polo team will, individually, be allowed to apply three swats apiece to your now TRULY bare posterior. Given the emphasis for both teams on upper body strength, I imagine they will wield The Corrector with even GREATER effect than did your class today. You should be WAILING LUSTILY long before they are through with you!

"Once their task is complete, I will have you released from the vaulting horse, sit down in the chair, turn you over my knee, and apply your delayed SIXTH HOUR SPANKING with The Facilitator with both teams and their coaches looking on. I suspect, given your recent experience with the paddle, the time it takes me to reduce you to KICKING AND TEARS will be quite brief indeed!

"Then, I will ONCE AGAIN parade you through the halls to your seventh period, SWATTING your rump on the count of 'one,' DISPLAY you ONCE AGAIN before your class, and ONCE AGAIN demand you apologize for your tardiness. Given that class, as I remember, is another section of freshman world history, I would suspect that the cadets therein may prove the most AMUSED of all, observing you as they will as BALD from your head to your toes as any eight year old. Even our the least mature cadet will manifest more signs of his manliness than YOU do."

The Commandant paused. He recalled that, in the seventh period class, there was a young man named Morrison. A tall, gangly boy with glasses, victim of a more than standard clumsiness as he got his growth, he was often the figure of fun of his fellow cadets and even of the faculty. And yet, Knighten had conceived a degree of affection for the kid, whom he happened to have whaled with The Facilitator about three weeks before for busting some equipment in the chemistry lab. He had taken his spanking with notable grit and resignation, though he had, of course, ended up SOBBING like all the rest.

Still, perhaps he deserved the opportunity to enjoy a fleeting moment of glory among his peers.

Knighten smiled. "I imagine, after punishing you SIX times in the course of the day, even if Cadet Steele, Cadet Green, or one of their fellows has relieved me at some point, MY energy and enthusiasm for BLISTERING your BARE BOTTOM will have begun to flag. Do not think for a MOMENT, however, that you will somehow escape further spanking in seventh hour. As I recall, there is a young man in that class by the name of Morrison..." At this point, Greene and Kelly both giggled. Doubtless both had been involved in some kind of hazing of the uncoordinated freshman. "...who, to my mind," the Commandant added pointedly, "will prove a great credit to both his class and Brownsfield Academy as his time here goes on. In any case, I will then invite Cadet Morrison to come to the front of the room to ONCE AGAIN turn you over HIS knee, and ONCE AGAIN employ The Facilitator to SPANK YOU TO TEARS before his fellow students before you begin the day's lesson. Despite his youth, I am CERTAIN he will fulfill his duty with great credit."

Knighten sighed. "When I determine he has, indeed, applied the hairbrush to your BARE BUTTOCKS in the way you DESERVE, I will ask Cadets Steele and Green to lift you from his lap and restrain you, bent over before the class. I will then SPREAD your RED and HAIRLESS behind to DISPLAY your anus to your class. At that point, as VIVID REMINDER to you of its power, I will INSERT the HANDLE of The Facilitator into your rectum." He sighed. "I regret it is NOT as large as the trophy presently lodged in your behind, which seems to have evoked a QUITE POWERFUL and, if I may say so, PLEASURED response from you. Still, I think the brush's handle will serve to evoke a not dissimilar reaction. You will be required to teach your class while retaining the shaft in your anus, with the head of the brush in FULL view of all. Given your condition today, I suppose you will be doing so with a NOTABLE erection, which should prove even MORE obvious emerging from you ENTIRELY SMOOTH crotch!"

"I need not add, I assume, that should you fail in this responsibility and allow the brush to drop to the floor, you will be SPANKED AGAIN by me or one of the cadets, the handle will be REINSERTED, and you will begin your lesson once again. The sight of you in this condition, Mr. Belknaps—the hairbrush PROTRUDING from between your ROSY buttocks and your THROBBING penis PROTRUDING before you--may provide the occasion for yet FURTHER amusement from your class, but, as before, that is YOUR problem, not mine, and I expect you to maintain an ORDERLY and DISCIPLINED atmosphere despite your condition, or FURTHER punishment will be in store for you!" His voice rose. "In sum, Mr. Belknaps, you have today ACTED like a juvenile, been PUNISHED like a juvenile, RESPONDED like a juvenile, and so, at Brownfield Academy, you will in the future both LOOK LIKE and be TREATED like a juvenile!

"After the schoolday is done, I will ask Cadets Steele and Green to accompany you to my office once again, employing their BELTS to WHIP your buttocks on the count of "one" as you are marched through the hall. You will then stand at parade rest by my door until 1700 hours, IN THE NUDE, of course, your RED BOTTOM a STRONG reminder of THIS INSTITUTION'S dim view of tardiness."

At this point, the Commandant paused. "This treatment will be your lot for the remainder of the week. You will be STRIPPED each morning and SPANKED before each class. And, remember, Mr. Belknaps," he added menacingly, "ANY sign of insubordination in the future during your tenure at this institution will be dealt with IMMEDIATELY in EXACTLY this same fashion!"

He then chuckled again. "Of course, should you choose NOT to return to your position tomorrow, a simple letter of resignation via the U. S. Mail will suffice."

He turned to the cadets. Certainly, he had given them an experience that would be ENGRAVED in their memories ever after. He looked out on his muscular, clean-shaven, young charges—the sweat-soaked Steele and Green, red-headed Kelly, curly-topped Newman, the always dedicated Lansdowne, and the rest. What a FINE and VALUABLE LESSON they had been given today. How, years and years from now, these manly young men would recall where they TRULY LEARNED of the PARTICULAR POWER of HARD and TRADITIONAL SPANKING!

"Gentlemen!" The Commandant bellowed, "You are dis-MISSED!"

The boys of Brownsfield Academy scampered away—Landsdown with his video, Kelly with his Polaroids, Newman with his photos for the 'net. The others dashed toward the drugstore to see if they could get 1 hour processing, each anxious to be the FIRST to show at home or work, in the barracks, to brothers and buddies and girlfriends and utter strangers the PHOTOGRAPHIC EVIDENCE of the INCREDIBLE events to which they had been witness!

Toby Steele and Mike Green, as one man, STREAKED out the front door. They knew exactly where they were headed, making a BEELINE for the two huge blue trash bins that sat by the blank wall by the mess hall. The two squeezed into narrow space between and, they were well aware, utterly out of public view, UNZIPPED their flies and allowed their PULSING PRONGS to POP into the open air.

It frankly took little more than a half-dozen strokes with their horny hands before both dicks DISGORGED vast loads of STEAMING CUM! Heavy gobs SPLATTED against the rusty metal and STAINED the ancient brick of the Academy. Steele's spunk was almost a STEADY STREAM as he PUMPED his PROBE, as Greene's joyjuice DROPPED and DRIBBLED in CRAZY patterns on the asphalt. The two cadets SHOT and SHOT, again and again, their BALLS simply BOILING OVER with the accumulated SEMEN of the SEXIEST SCENE they had either SEEN or PARTICIPATED IN their entire lives!

It seemed they SPEWED for minutes on end, their RANDY reamers ROCKED by SPASM after SPASM. They were both COMPLETELY out of breath, gasping for air, and exhausted when the last of their loads leaked from the slits of their CROWING COCKS! Their knees were weak, and shudders QUAKED through their STURDY frames.

"Man!" Steele managed to croak. "This was absolutely the HOTTEST day of my whole fuckin' LIFE!"

"You know it!" Green panted. "Who'd've THOUGHT that SPANKING was such a TURN-ON!"

They leaned against the trash bin, still winded.

"Janet better get used to going over my knee," Steel said, "because I'm gonna WARM her little BUTT every time I PLOW her, that's for sure."

"Mandy, too," Greene smiled. "I LOVE porkin' that cute little rear end of hers anyhow, and, from now on, it's gonna be HOT PINK when it takes my STICK!"

"Hey, let's call 'em! We missed practice anyhow. Commandant's orders!" Steele grinned. "Maybe we could get both our chicks down in the woods TOGETHER for a little afternoon delight!

"And a BIG surprise!" Mike added.

"Yeah. They won't know what's comin' when we pull those panties down! POW!"

"Sounds good to me! Got change?"

The two began their journey to the payphone on the corner. Both were smiling still.

"You know, man..." Steele began, "I was thinkin'. After today, maybe we ought to do a little 'revising' in our TEAM initiations in the spring, too."

"Yeah," Greene nodded enthusiastically. "I can think of a few frosh dickheads goin' out for track that would fit REAL nice over my lap!"

"I'd love to see what color Chen's ass turns when you lay a hairbrush on it," Steele agreed. "And what about that new guy, that cocksucker junior, Portman. He's almost as hairy as Furball. HEY, maybe we ought to SHAVE his rear before we SPANK it!"

"I'd want to make him BAWL, dude. He's such an asshole."

The two stopped in their tracks and looked at each other. They both knew what the other was thinking.

"Ya know, speaking of assholes," Steele said casually, "as long as we got those boys BAREBUTT, maybe we oughta make 'em let us PRONG their little PUCKERS, too."

Green smirked. "Yeah. REALLY do some REAMIN'! After all, whippin' butt-- BRISKLY and VIGOROUSLY--can really give a man one POWERFUL BONER!"

Toby Steele giggled. "You got THAT right, dude!"

Guffawing all the way, the two gridiron stars continued toward the phone.

Meanwhile, in the foyer of Brownsfield Academy, Ned Belknaps heard a single set of footsteps. It was Sergeant Pierce, who laid Ned's pants on the radiator and, painstakingly, untied Ned's tie that bound him to the steampipe. Had he had the strength, Ned might have punched him, but his legs were of rubber, and his ass, of course, was still ABLAZE. Besides, Pierce had not been his tormentor—well, with the exception of 10 swats, anyway. And what was 10 swats in the sum of the number of blows his butt had endured?

Upon releasing him, Pierce walked away without a word and locked the door to the office.

Ned slipped on his spitty shorts. JESUS CHRIST! He could hardly stand the contact of the cotton on his ravaged rump! He'd have to drive home standing up! But he persevered, and put his trousers on. He ripped the DUNCE cap from his head, and stomped on it. He had already removed the ballbat from his asshole. He had wound the ribbon around his finger, and, at first, tried to GENTLY urge the probing POLE from his pouty pucker.

But his rectum resisted, holding tight to STOUT STICK planted deep within it. In the end, he had RIPPED the improvised dildo from his rear with one powerful YANK. The sudden VOID inside him had been one of the STRANGEST sensations Ned Belknaps had ever felt, an ACHING EMPTINESS in his gut he had never known. With his finger, he could tell his ANUS was GAPING and GRASPING, as if it actually DESIRED that 8" ram were once again there to STRETCH and STROKE it.

Ned brought the trophy around to look at it. Good God, it was BIG! STICKY and SHINY with his own ASSJUICE, it SHIMMERED in the dying light of day as he studied it.

Then, suddenly, he cocked his arm and sent it PINWHEELING down the hall to clatter to the floor near the turn toward his classroom.

He had little time to lose. If, on the one hand, the Commandant's threat for next day seemed ABSURD in its intensity, Ned was perfectly aware that, having made such a public announcement, Knighten would make good on it, regardless of the cost. He had NO desire to test the Commandant's will. He was leaving--TONIGHT! There could be no returning to Brownsfield Academy. He would go far, far away and begin again.

And so, with BLISTERED BOTTOM SOUNDLY SPANKED, out the door Ned Belknaps made his solitary way.

So ends what became known as "THE INCIDENT AT BROWNSFIELD ACADEMY, or THE TEACHER'S HORRIBLE HUMILIATION..."

POSTSCRIPT

As might be expected, "The Incident"—as it came to be referred to--had a significant and lasting effect on many of its participants, witnesses, and even upon those who had not been directly involved. It became, needless to say, an instant legend at Brownsfield Academy. Almost immediately and even moreso in years following, the events of that fateful day were recounted, embellished, expanded, exaggerated, deformed, and otherwise altered for emphasis in accord with the particular fascinations of whomever told the story. Those cadets who had merely been observers of the astonishing scene, over time, invented their own roles in Mr. Belknaps' ongoing humiliation, and as the years passed, they came to believe their own fictions, relating in great detail how they themselves had had the teacher over their knees, how he had in fact returned the following day and been subjected to the discipline The Commandant had so lovingly described, and so on. Even some who entered Brownsfield after the by-now - mythic occurrence invented scenarios in which, by some fluke—a campus tour, a visit to an older brother, a happenstance trip to the Academy to retrieve some brochure or form—they had ended up taking part in what was, to be sure, the most historic day in the history of the institution.

Nonetheless, the "impact," as it were, of "The Incident" upon some of the members of the Brownsfield community can, in fact, be verified, and so, in the interests of full-disclosure, here appended are the tales of various of those who played a part in the days' events.

THE STAFF:

Ned Belknaps was never spanked again in his life.

Having made a precipitous escape from the entire region (by dawn the next day he was three states distant), he took a month to gather his dignity and to allow his backside to return to its natural and unblemished state. No one was more astonished than he at the rapidity of his recovery. Within a week, aside from some deep bruises, his rear end was more or less back to normal, aside from the incriminating "**BAD BOY**" written across his cheeks. Within two weeks, all traces of his ordeal had vanished. With that, he came to understand the awesome resilience of the male bottom. Little wonder it had been employed for millennia as the site of punishment. Certainly, no other part of the body could absorb such sustained abuse and, within a relatively short time, regain its natural suppleness, softness, and color.

After various inquiries, after Christmas, Ned Belknaps moved as far away as he could go, to Hawaii. The paradisical islands were a far cry indeed from the gloomy precincts of Brownsfield Academy. There, he found a job in a progressive high school he quite enjoyed, an institution—obviously—that had no tradition of corporal punishment.

Not long after, he married again, and was a model husband and parent.

Of course, he could never forget the Incident at Brownsfield Academy. Even years later, he would, on occasion, encounter to his terrific embarrassment pictures of himself, red-bottomed and dunce capped, on the 'net late at night. In the world of spanking, his was one of the most famous fannies in the world. The photographs, Polaroids, and digital shots snapped that day appeared on endless websites on every continent, his swollen, blazing rumpus and tear-strained face the object of comments in languages he did not even understand—*"Quel fesse!"* *"Que culo recastigado*!" "Man, this dude is wailin'!" One evening, he even saw what seemed the videotape of his thrashing at the hands of Steele and Green. There, in an endless loop, Ned watched—a hot blush on his face--his bare bottom dance and spasm beneath the merciless assault of the two sweating seniors, his shorts-muffled cries echoing over the laughter of the uniformed boys observing and recording his punishment. It brought the whole horrific experience back for him, though, at the same time, he could barely bring himself to look away from his own half-naked figure bouncing like a mad marionette on the screen. How he squirmed! How his backside glowed!

More significantly, however, he found (first with horror, then with resignation, ultimately with pleasure) that he recalled nostalgically the feel of that ball bat thrust up his rectum. The ongoing erection he had maintained despite the battering of his buns demonstrated powerfully his profound enjoyment of deep anal stimulation. He recognized that, though primarily straight, there was a bisexual part of him that truly enjoyed a good, hard fucking up the ass.

With time, having grown comfortable with his realization, he confided in his wife. To his relief, she was quite understanding, and, to his thrilled surprise, revealed to him her own occasional urges toward women. From that point on, they enjoyed a even better and more satisfying sex life. Many was the time Ned screwed his mate with a large buttplug she had obtained planted firmly up his anus. They joined a "Banging Bi's" group, and Ned found, at their get-togethers, he truly loved occasionally seeing his wife getting her muff expertly eaten by another woman while he lazily stroked his dick, just as she enjoyed seeing her husband on his hands and knees, grunting and groaning with lust as he was royally reamed from behind by another man's cock.

Once a month, they would settle the kids with her parents and then go their separate ways. Ned would often take off on camping trips with a group of like-minded, mostly married men of all ages who, amid the spectacular tropical scenery, would pass the weekend enjoying each other's bodies. He learned the delights of pleasuring another guy's dick, balls, and ass with his mouth, and, of course, had his own cock and butt serviced similarly. He developed something of a reputation as well as an excellent rump reamer, perhaps because he himself found so much relief in getting his own anus stirred and stretched. On occasion, he had two of the fellows on hands and knees before him, furry rumps spread wide, and he would bang one ass for a while, fingering the other gently, then withdraw, eat out the fingered asshole while diddling the one recently fucked, then jam his cock up the saliva-sweetened pucker while drumming three fingers on walls of the rectum which had so recently housed his poker in its glove-like grip.

Still, getting his own butt fucked remained his greatest pleasure, and his rear end was quite a favorite among his cohorts.

In these get-togethers, before dawn, Ned would sometimes wander naked from his tent before dawn and bend and spread on all fours in the middle of the campsite to offer his hole to all comers as they awoke, taking as many as six or eight rammers one after another up his maletwat. He would remain in that position the entire day, his rump in the air, cheeks splayed apart, his pucker winking an invitation to any cock anxious to drill his randy rectum. His fellow campers would come and go, knowing, whenever they felt the urge, Ned's rump was available for a good pounding. When not getting plowed, he found himself in an almost Zen-like state--tremendously aware of his body, of the breezes wafting over him ruffling his butthairs, the rich, tropical smells of the island's vegetation. He would rub his face on the earth, feeling a wonderful oneness with nature as seed dribbled from his asshole and coursed slowly—man-honey—down his thighs. Those days, he would remain with his own dick dripping, not even wanting to come, dreamy and almost delirious with the sensations the gangbangs, the individual reamings, the rimmings and other assplay evoked in his insides.

Occasionally, on these outings, a spanking or paddling would be administered, but Ned only watched. He did come to understand just how stimulating this activity could be, observing a male ass bounce and jiggle and grow redder and redder as it was soundly smacked, seeing toes dance on the ground and then feet pumping the air wildly, hearing manly grunts and groans turn to "Ows! and "Ouches! before finally resolving into full-throated boyish bawling. A couple of the other men seemed to truly enjoy getting turned across another's knee for a sound rumproasting. He could understand the need of one of his furry, buff, and burly cohorts to surrender to another of their number and get spanked to the point of tears and finally reaching some magical point of regression where they squalled: "Oh, Daddy! Daddy! I'm so, so sorry I was a bad boy! Spank me, Daddy! Spank all the badness out of me!"

But Ned never indulged in such games. "The Incident" had, sadly, closed off that particular avenue of pleasure for him. If invited to take part, he would politely decline, smiling mysteriously, thinking always: "If you only knew…!"

Sergeant Pierce got his bare bottom spanked regularly by the Commandant during the entire five years he remained at Brownsfield Academy. After "The Incident," if anything, the spankings increased in frequency and intensity. With the punishment of Ned Belknaps, the Commandant's expectations of the proper results of a sound thrashing obviously grew, stripping his assistant of pants and underpants entirely and continuing the discipline of Pierce's's exposed posterior until the younger man was reduced at the end to the frantic kicking and blubbering tears of an ill-mannered eight year old, very sorry for his misdeeds.

It was about three months after the incident that Mr. Knighten introduced a new wrinkle into his punishment of his assistant. The sergeant was never informed why the Commandant decided further embarrassment should be in order for him. It was simply that, one day, he reported to his boss's office to find that the head of maintenance, a powerfully built African-American in his forties named Wallace Rose, had been invited to attend his dressing-down.

Rose was initially amazed and then quite amused by Pierce's pants down predicament, and even more so by the humiliating and painful process that followed as the Sergeant's lily-white, grown-up ass was transformed into the well-blistered bootie of a naughty little boy. When Pierce began his desperate "backwards can can"—feet flying in every direction—and wailed out pleas and promises to The Commandant, Rose erupted into knee-slapping guffaws!

From that point, the Sergeant often found himself disciplined not once but twice—first by the Commandant, then by Rose, who favored The Facilitator and found he quite enjoyed releasing the numerous frustrations of his job on the wildly wiggling fanny of a caterwauling countryboy beneath the Commandant's watchful eye, turning what was already a shocking pink behind a blazing red. Rose spanked hard! Pierce could count on bawling twice as loud and long when sprawled over the well-muscled black man's knee.

The Commandant, as well, seemed to enjoy watching his subaltern forced into a frantic lapdance by the school janitor. Though he himself blistered bare bottoms with great frequency, his opportunities to enjoy the satisfying spectacle of true and humiliating discipline as an observer were few. Watching Pierce's hairy hindparts jump and yaw as that hairbrush did its stinging work was a delight, and the sound of the Sergeant's howls and the ever-changing expressions of pain and shame upon the younger man's face were, to The Commandant, sheer poetry.

Just after his thirty-fourth birthday, Sergeant Pierce abruptly moved back to Tennessee, where he married and fathered children. Though he would occasionally threaten to "take off his belt," he in fact never employed corporal punishment in his family, all too aware of the stimulation he had felt the day he had watched the Commandant spank Ned Belknaps. Indeed, his sudden departure was precipitated by his realization—late one night as he applied Intensive Care Cream to his well-blistered backside--that he himself had actually begun to anticipate and enjoy his discipline at the hands of The Commandant and

Wallace Rose.

Mr. Paine and **Mr. Slopes**, both married, were not long able to keep the condition of their backsides a secret from their wives after their monthly "performance reviews." Both women were initially shocked, though also found themselves strangely intrigued. They mutually discussed the matter, and were surprised they had each observed how their husbands' concentration on their jobs did indeed seem to increase after their visits those Saturdays to the basement of Brownsfield Academy. It did not take long for them to become interested in the concept of punishing their husbands themselves for careless or thoughtless behavior.

They discovered a chatgroup of "disciplinary wives" and, not long after, a number of publications devoted to the notion of "women in charge." They became part of a community who adhered to the philosophy that most men remained nothing but little boys at heart, and consequently required the kind of correction little boys were traditionally subject to.

Thenceforth, the hapless German instructor and his equally unfortunate colleague in physics found themselves getting their trousers lowered not only once a month at school, but far more frequently at home!

Mrs. Paine obtained a razor strop with which she regularly set her spouse's furry, beefy backside on fire when he failed to take out the trash or forgot her request for something from the market. Mr. Slope's hairless heinie fared no better after his wife demanded he make her a powerful paddle and, on a weekly basis, lowered his drawers and took him over her lap on the bed to tan his twitching tail for the "demerits" he inevitably accumulated over the preceding seven days, of which Mrs. Slopes kept assiduous record. These ranged from the major ("tardiness" or "sassing"), to the more subtle (a badly folded dishtowel; leaving the toilet seat up).

Both men assented meekly, perhaps even willingly, to their new situation as "overgrown boys," though they learned to dread even more their "reviews" at home and school. Those Saturdays, after the Commandant was done with them, they would find themselves at one of their houses or the other, the both of them dressed in T-shirts, short pants, sweat socks, and sneakers, baseball caps planted backwards on their heads like the merest 12 year olds, wearing not their usual boxers but boy's briefs. The children would have been safely packed away with a babysitter elsewhere. It was not long, of course, before they both had their trousers and underpants lowered and stood bare-bottomed before their strict wives, their backsides already sore and reddened by the Commandant.

"Boys who get spanked at school," the women would say, "obviously then have to be spanked at home!"

There followed multiple rumproastings for both men that always resulted in kicking and tears! Mrs. Paine would—expertly and fiercely--lay the strop across her husband's ample ass as he bent over the back of a chair and blubbed his increasingly desperate promises to be of greater help around the house, while, simultaneously, Mrs. Slopes administered stern lessons in "applied psychology" to her squirming spouse's rumpus with her paddle as, sprawled across her lap on the sofa, he sobbed assurances he would spend more time with the kids. On occasion, Mrs. Paine would invite Mrs. Slopes to paddle her spouse's already reddened rear, and Mrs. Slopes, of course, would return the favor by asking Mrs. Paine to administered "a sound stropping" across her husband's already blistered behind.

Not only spankings, but corner time, writing lines, and mouth soapings for their backtalk--along with such other juvenile reminders as rectal temperatures and warm, soapy enemas--were both men's lots those days, their tender hindparts so thoroughly ravaged by the time both their boss and their wives were through with them they not only slept on their tummies on Saturday nights but spent the entire Sunday following standing up!

Still, many of the other women in the area would marvel at how kind and thoughtful Mrs. Paine's and Mrs. Slopes' husbands were, little suspecting either the means by which they were kept in line, or the inspiration for it.

THE CADETS:

Impressionable young men that they were at the time, the Incident at Brownsfield Academy proved a seminal event, to coin a phrase, for many of the cadets. A large number moved on to the armed services, there to make their lives, and many, when they had families, unsurprisingly proved strict disciplinarians, employing bare bottom spankings as a matter of course, even with their adolescent children. Of course, given they themselves had been subject to this kind of punishment at such an age, this is not especially surprising. Amundsen, Eggbert, Hansen, Landsdowne, and many others grew up committed MEN WHO SPANK!.

A few of the cadets, however, merit special attention.

Selwyn, ever the good soldier, spent ten years in the Marine Corps. Upon his discharge, however, he found himself adrift. He tried several careers, but none seemed to work out, and ultimately found himself working as a "male maid" though a temporary service in a middle-sized Midwestern city.

There, happily, fate took a hand. One of his assignments was to clean the home of one Rod Vernor, the owner of the local leather bar, "The Stick," who was impressed with Selwyn's good work habits, his good looks, tight body, and polite demeanor. He offered Selwyn a position as his houseboy and personal assistant. Though he made clear that this job would involve a wide variety of duties, and that he was a firm believer in "traditional discipline," Selwyn eagerly accepted.

Thus it was that Selwyn's wardrobe from then on consisted largely of a collection of jockstraps, thongs, bikini briefs, extraordinarily skimpy shorts cut high in the back, athletic socks, and boots whether at home or at the bar. Cooking, cleaning, keeping the books, tending bar when called upon—his pert, swimmer's rump was on constant display, and often cherry red as well. For Selwyn, any dereliction of duty meant a good, hard spanking from "the boss," and then some time in corner to consider his misdeed before he returned to work, even on the busiest Friday and Saturday nights at The Stick. Indeed, weekend business at the bar seemed to increase as word spread in the community that "the cute, blond bartender" might find himself slung over the bar, upended over a stool, or yanked across Ron Vernor's lap for a firm application of hand, strap, or paddle to his pert and very naked behind.

One might think that Selwyn would object, at his age, to his ongoing spankings at the hands of his employer, and he did, at first, express certain reservations. Rod made clear, however, that bare bottom blisterings were part of the job description, period. An astute judge of men, Ron added that, obviously, Selwyn missed the structure and discipline he had flourished under at Brownsfield Academy and in the Corps.

"But, golly, Mr. Vernor, they didn't beat my butt in the Marines!"

Ron surveyed Selwyn up and down. "Maybe they should have, dude. Maybe you'd have made your twenty years then."

And that, apparently, settled it. What his boss said made a great deal of sense to Selwyn. Looking back, his performance in life had never been better than it had been at Brownsfield, with the threat of The Corrector or The Facilitator always hanging over his head—or rear! And, though he had loved the service, he hadn't been as successful as he might have wished. Maybe if only the Sergeant had spanked him!

Certainly, since he re-entered civilian life, his record had been far from stellar. Maybe he was simply the kind of guy who needed to be physically knocked down a peg or two on a regular basis to live up to his full potential.

From that point on, Selwyn submitted to his punishments, if not with enthusiasm, with good grace, convinced that Ron Vernor did indeed have his best interests at heart, even if it meant an extremely red, sore bottom!

Also, over time, under his boss's guidance, Selwyn became a very respectable cocksucker, regularly servicing his employer whenever asked. Beyond this, he would, without question, "bend over and spread" when so ordered, so as to take the dick of Vernor or whomever else Vernor so designated up his asshole. After hours at The Stick often found Selwyn naked on hands and knees on the pool table with his already red bottom in the air, servicing the cocks of his boss's special clients. He considered all these simply part of his job, and learned not only to accept but to enjoy them.

When asked, however, he would insist he was, in fact, straight, and, though he did not marry, often dated. Some women were shocked, but he found many who did not seem to mind the requirements of his career. He was, after all, an attractive man with a fine member of his own and quite adept in bed. On a few occasions, one girlfriend or another came to The Stick after hours to watch her boyfriend service the customers, and found it quite stimulating.

As one might expect, if the topic of his spankings and use by other men came up, he would say, simply, that, when he was giving head or getting fucked or squirming over his boss's knee in front of the patrons of The Stick, he was "just following orders."

Marxbury, as "house pussy," was indeed fucked within an inch of his life the night following Mr. Belknaps' spanking. Every boarder without exception lined up that evening to use either his mouth or hole, including some who had never before invoked their privileges during the "designated hour." Within the week, as he had dreaded, Kelly and Chen succeeded in "double-teaming" his ass, and, given their delighted description of the sensation of two cocks gripped by a single butthole, it soon was not at all unusual for Marxbury to find himself on his back getting his throat rammed while two cadet dicks roiled and rolled around in his thoroughly stretched rectum.

Not even his hopes of avoiding the pain of spanking were realized. It was Amundsen who remembered The Commandant's passing remark about a "willow switch" when he thrashed Ned Belknaps with the pointer, and it was not long before a number were cut, smoothed, and bundled in a secret spot beneath the floorboards. If a cadet felt Marxbury was not sucking his dick or worshipping his balls or asscrack to his satisfaction, another would retrieve a switch to apply some stinging "encouragement" to the hapless junior's round and frantically wiggling behind. A few of the boys—Landsdowne and Eggbert in particular—insisted Marxbury be switched while servicing their cocks, claiming his howling throat was deeper and more giving when his bottom was being lashed ferociously.

By graduation, Marxbury had accepted the fact that his classmates had converted him into a complete male whore. Simply looking at the crotch of another male's pants was enough to give this class pussy a woody and make his boytwat twitch in anticipation. Turning this to his advantage, he moved to Los Angeles, where he shaved his tight cadet body completely smooth and began frequenting the better known bars and bath houses. It did not take long for him to meet some interesting and well-connected friends, and, within a year, his talented mouth and insatiable and very desirable rump had earned him considerable renown in porn videos.

There, his squatty cock was no problem as he submitted to throat rammings and fannyfuckings of some of the most well-endowed studs in L.A. All were impressed with his capacity to take cock after massive cock one after another without complaint from either or both ends, which he freely admitted was the result of "intense military training." Spankings, of course, were very much part of his repertoire. To his directors, he would suggest ways tailtannings might be integrated into the action, and in any case, in his regular appearances as fuckee, would groan and growl at the stud porking his pucker: "Slap my ass! Yeah! Hard! Yeah! Harder! Make me grab that big fuckstick! Spank me!

With remarkable rapidity, Marxbury had a vast and loyal

following of porn viewers who clamored for new material featuring that incredible bottom--"Private Paul Ploud."

Within a year, Marxbury was joined, somewhat to his surprise, by his classmates **Vasquez** and **Arkanian**. The big-donged Chicano had always thoroughly enjoyed pounding male-cunt, while the beercan-hung Armenian shotputter had, after much internal struggle and denial, admitted to himself his own blossoming queerness. Tonguing and fucking a girl's pussy was okay, but there was nothing like slathering a guy's funky asshole with spit and then ramming his massive cock up a strangling male rumpring! He dated this discovery from that day in the classroom when his cock had helplessly responded to the sight of his teacher's spread and wiggling rear, especially that moment when he and Vasquez had been pulling Mr. Belknaps' legs apart and he had smelled the incredible aroma of male rump and felt an inexplicable desire to plant a deep kiss on that fiery butt.

Indeed, asswiping became his particular specialty, and many was the butt driven to a frenzy by his lips, teeth, and tongue's poking, licking, nipping attentions. Marxbury was able to find his two old friends employment in the adult entertainment industry as well, and so the two—as "Norberto Nailer" and (unsurprisingly) "Harry Rimmer'—joined Paul Ploud for epic and very lucrative sessions of male sex before the whirring cameras.

One very popular video—*Cadet Cum-Crammers*--featured the three classmates together, in uniform once again, though, needless to say, they were all in their skivvies within two minutes and buck naked within five. In an extended sequence, Arkanian slopped Marxbury's shaved anus with gallons of saliva as the smaller boy's own face bobbed wildly up and down on Vasquez's meaty manslab, taking it all the way down to those thick Mexican pubes. When Marxbury's pucker was finally pink and pouty with the lapping and drilling of the Armenian's tongue, the furry rimmer then mounted that pulsing boycunt—his massive tool seeming to stretch those spitty asslips to the limit—only to be eventually joined in that aching asshole by the Chicano's glimmering, well-sucked, and potent poker for a fabulous, never-before-seen double-fuck of over fifteen minutes on the video screens of individuals, baths, and bars all over the world.

Kelly and **Chen** enjoyed their barracks privileges with Marxbury's lips and ass with great enthusiasm till that particular house pussy's graduation. Then, ironically and to their horror, an extraordinarily well-endowed freshman class joined the ranks of Brownsfield Academy. Though they both sported a solid six inches between their legs, it was the freckled Irish boy and his Asian cohort who "came up short" in equal degree at the September measurement, and so spent the next year as "co-house pussies" themselves!

Much was the gagging before they learned to be decent cocksuckers. Deep was their disgust when they first found hairy, sweaty buttholes of their fellow boarders enthroned upon their faces. Both dreaded the sting of the switch on their wriggling rears as dripping dicks plugged their mouths, and how they had squealed when they lost their rump cherries to the prongs of two particularly long-donged newcomers who had, in a cutting of the cards, won the privilege of ravaging the two squirming virgins that first night at the designated hour. Still, both stoically accepted their places within the Academy's traditions, and provided good service to their bunkmates for the entire year following.

Chen, to his joy, was relieved of duties the following first term, thanks to the arrival of a massively built but interestingly small-dicked transfer named Galt, who himself actually seemed to enjoy his responsibilities to the cocks and slimslits of his barracks buds. Years later, many was the cadet who, as he pronged his wife or sweetheart, secretly recalled the remarkable ministrations of Galt's astonishing tongue and downy and well-muscled rump on their randy rods. Chen chalked up his experience to the indiscretions of his youth, married, and had kids. He moved on to a notable career in the Army, where, interestingly, his relatively lax enforcement of the "don't ask, don't tell" policy occasionally made other officers wonder about his own past.

But Chen never tipped his hand.

Kelly's story is very different. He remained a lifelong bachelor. As it happened, one of his brothers had noted, when he was home on a weekend pass, the tell-tale marks of the switch on his fanny, and Kelly had unwisely confided their origin, along with his other duties in the dorm. Though he did not know it, that knowledge was soon shared with his other brothers.

Hence, upon his graduation, when he joined the family business—a transmission service—his brothers made it clear they would expect, upon demand, the same services for themselves he had so willingly provided to his classmates! And a horny crew these Irish boys were! Hardly a day went by at the shop that Kelly was not dragged to the "private office" in back to be fucked fore and aft by at least a couple of his brothers both older and younger, while those typical weekend boys' get-togethers for beer and sports found him naked and on all fours in the den of his eldest brother's house as all his male siblings lustily porked him front and back when the game was slow.

During baseball season, the term "seventh inning stretch" took on a whole new meaning for Kelly's asshole!

It took no time, to Kelly's horror, for his brothers to discover the joys of spanking as a kind of foreplay, and so he would find himself with his pants down, his freckled fanny turning violent pink as it bucked and bounced across a manly knee and his feet flew frantically in the air before he was soundly fucked. He spent his entire life with a bottom with a permanent blush, not to mention a well-used deep throat and a perpetually reamed rectum.

With the years, certain cousins and, later, even nephews and a few select customers were let in on the secret and took advantage of Kelly's by now thoroughly-trained and quite talented holes when they were horny or their wives were pregnant or girlfriends were out of town. Kelly, ever loyal, eventually accepted his place in the family scheme of things, and would think now and then of "The Incident," perhaps most vividly one weekend almost twenty years later.

Then, a brawny eighteen year old cousin, Sean, only recently inducted in this particular family tradition, had turned Kelly pantless across his knee and proceeded to blister his bottom blazing red with a wooden hairbrush, this to the cheers and jeers of the laughing multitude of the assembled Irishmen of all ages before Kelly was mercilessly gangbanged for the next four hours. Wailing and flailing across that broad-shouldered boy's steely thighs, his socks a blur and his bottom on fire, Kelly felt he finally understood, at least to a point, what it must have been for Ned Belknaps to bawl and buck across The Commandant's lap in the classroom as he got a hard, bare bottom, hairbrush spanking before those young cadets all those years before.

Janet and **Mandy**, the girlfriends respectively of Toby Steele and Mike Green, were none too pleased to find themselves in the woods the very afternoon of "The Incident"—skirts up, panties down, squirming and squealing as their boyfriends introduced their pear-shaped fannies to their newly discovered interest in spanking. Neither girl ever learned to enjoy that particular game, but both accepted the smack of the football players' massive palms across their stinging girlrumps as the price to be paid for the satisfaction provided by the two boys powerful shafts, which seemed to swell to even greater length and girth after warming the young ladies' hindparts.

Still, Steele and Green took it easy on their girlfriends' bottoms, for the most part, reserving their more muscular swats for the naked rears of other jocks at Brownsfield Academy. Neither played basketball or hockey, but the initiation for that year's swimming and track teams provided ample opportunity to introduce the freshly minted tradition of old-fashioned blistering as part of the hazing for the new members of the squad. Many was the tearful neophyte that evening as Steele and Green, with other established stars, whaled their flailing male rearcheeks not just with their hands, but their belts and straps (including a fanbelt from a local auto supply store), numerous switches from trees of different varieties (birch, hickory, willow, and so on), a variety of paddles picked up at the bookstore of a nearby university which stocked them for their local fraternities, a couple of shower brushes from the local dollar store, and even an old rattan rugbeater Green discovered in his grandmother's basement. Bent-over, across the knee, on all fours, sprawled across chairs, tables, desks, and sofas, track team tail twisted and tossed and swimmer-rump bucked and bounced as upperclassman toasted the tushes off the unfortunate newcomers. Sprinters or discus-throwers, hurdlers or high jumpers, sidestrokers or butterfly champions, it mattered not—all rears were royally roasted that chilly February night.

That was not all. Not a single recent addition to the squad retained his male virginity front or back. Each throat was violated by the steely shaft of at least one classmate, while no butt-cherry remained unbroken by rampaging student studpole. Further, both Schick and Gillette saw a rise in sales as the initiates—from furriest Italian to glassiest-bodied blond—found himself deprived of every shred of manly hair in crotch, on balls and asses. Steele and Green took great delight in subjecting a teary-eyed and blazing-bottomed Portman to this treatment after they had both spanked him soundly, before then placing him on hands and knees—Steele before him and Green to the rear—to plough and pound the hapless junior's baby-face and now baby-smooth ass without pause with their randy dicks.

The new rites of spring initiations were immediately adopted by every other team at Brownsfield Academy, and so it was that no jock cadet ever left the school with an unblemished bottom or without the knowledge of the ravishments a meaty prong may extract from mouth and asshole.

Such was the ironic legacy of Ned Belknaps and the "Incident at Brownsfield Academy."

Steele and **Green** themselves graduated that spring and went on to college and then military careers—Steele in the Marine Corps and Green in the Navy. After a few wild and woolly bachelor years, they married and had children. Both proved strict disciplinarians with both their boys and their girls, their fatherly hands and later belts and hairbrushes imposing swift and painful justice on the wiggling and always bare bottoms of their kids.

However, they did indulge in one ritual that might have surprised their spouses and others who knew then.

Once a year after graduation, the two would retreat to Green's parent's vacation home, an isolated cabin deep in the woods. But they were not alone. They would scan the ads of local underground papers or the internet to encounter males who identified themselves as "slaves." One lucky (?) such indvidual would be chosen to serve these two horny military men, who from Friday night to late Sunday afternoon, extracted a year's worth of their desires on the body of their "bad boy." Endless spankings, hours of buttfuckings, constant blowjobs, ongoing asskissing, along with devilish games with rubber gloves, buttplugs, dildos, vibrators, and other toys Steele and Green had picked up over the year were the lot of the hapless maletwat—shaved from the top of his head to the fur on his toes—they had elected to serve them. There were those who, at the end of their servitude, hoped never again to lay eyes on their stern and tireless military masters, though there were a few who, on their knees of course, begged when the weekend was over to please be considered as next year's naked object of lust.

Then, one particular March, a sudden snowstorm prevented the slave from arriving! Steele and Green found themselves, alone and isolated in the cabin with flint-hard, weeping dicks, and no outlet for their dominant desires.

"Well," Toby Steel smirked, "I guess we'll just have to figure things out between the two of us."

"Wh-wh-what do you mean?" Green stammered nervously.

"One of us'll just have to be the scumbag, dude. Let's just cut the cards and see who loses and get on with it." Steele laughed confidently, eying Mike's tail tight in his pants.

"I don't know…"

"Chicken?"

"No!" Green snapped, though sweat had begun to form on his forehead and upper lip.. "Okay."

Steele shuffled the deck and set it in the middle of the coffee table.

"Cut."

"No. You first."

"All right." Toby took a stack and turned it over. He grinned. "Jack of spades."

Green gulped. He could already feel the hardwood hairbrush stinging his bouncing bottom, and his friend's massive tool invading his untried rectum, which had never had anything bigger up it than a doctor's finger.

"So..."

"Okay, okay." Mike cut...

Held the cards for a moment...

Turned them over.

It was his turn to smile.

"Drop those pants, slaveboy!" Mike Green barked. "King of diamonds!"

And it was diamonds that Toby Steele saw all that weekend, as his friend subjected him to the treatment they two of them had, over the years, so lustily imposed on other males. Toby's legs windmilled wildly in the air as he cried his eyes out while Mike mercilessly spanked his bouncing buttocks again and again with the wooden hairbrush, his leather belt, a cedar paddle. He swallowed what seemed like gallons of cum from his buddy's apparently tireless balls, gagging as his throat was ploughed raw. His burning and now hairless behind was mercilessly reamed again and again by Green's rockhard pussyrammer, and he learned the taste and smell and texture of a Navyman's furry rump and funky anus as he rimmed out Mike's tight slimslit for what seemed hours. He learned to bow and serve with a major buttplug twisted into his rectum, and clean between the toes of his old friend with his exhausted tongue.

What was most amazing of all, however, was what happened late Saturday night, as Green once again paddled the fanny off the crying and hapless Marine with a pingpong paddle—"WAA-AAAHHH!! SIR! PLE-EEAASSEE!!! WAA-AA-AAAHHHH!!"--then slammed his throbbing manpole between the fiery cheeks of his erstwhile chum. As he porked that by now well-drilled anus, Toby Steele suddenly began to shout: "Oh, fuck me! Fuck me, Sir! Oh, fuck my pussy! Fuck me till I can't walk. Oh, yes, Sir! Yes, Sir! Harder! Harder! Fuuu-uucckkk mmmeeeee!!"

At that instant, Green suddenly poured a huge load of gyzm into Steele's grasping asshole, then yanked his dick out.

"NNOOOOOO!" Toby squealed.

He turned frantically toward Green and, inserting three thick fingers up his own burning and throbbing rear in a fruitless attempt to replace the fullness of the sailor's dick, fell to his knees and absorbed Green's softening prong in his mouth, chowing down on that manly meat smothered with his own buttjuice as he desperately diddled his own rectum, his head bobbing up and down. Within seconds, his own stiff probe began to helplessly spew wad after wad of whitehot gyzm all over the floor.

And at that moment, both those alumni of the Incident at Brownsfield Academy were speechless. They realized something astonishing, something amazing: at heart, the implacable spanker and buttfucker Toby Steele himself was, in fact, a born boyslave.

"Aw right!" Green growled, jamming his rammer and half his ballsack into Toby's mouth. "Get my dong hard again before I blister the bejesus out of that bottom of yours, asswipe! And then I'm gonna ream your piggy-ass till you walk like a girl!"

Thus, in their meetings that followed, it was Major Toby Steele who found himself red-faced and red-bottomed with a ravaged throat and a raw rectum, the blistered-ass scumbag of Captain Mike Green. On a couple of occasions, Green, in fact, allowed his buddy to turn him over his knee, just to see what it was like. Indeed, he once ordered Toby to take his asscherry (a rare privilege for any slaveboy!), though this subsequently resulted in a switching of Steele's behind that left him wailing like a baby even as he begged to be thrashed even harder.

Steele's desire to be used was so intense that the yearly meetings became quarterly, then monthly if they could be arranged, as he pleaded with his old friend again and again to make him into his personal spank-and-fuck toy!

Of the tales of Brownfield alumni who were witness to "The Incident," that of the scrappy wrestler, **Newman**, is perhaps the most instructive and inspirational. Among those cadets who took part in the punishment and humiliation of Ned Belknaps, his role would seem to have been a relatively minor one compared to that of Selwyn or of Steele and Green. And yet, "The Incident" may, in fact, have had a greater impact on his later life in a most positive way than it did on any of his fellows.

During "The Incident," it was Newman who compiled perhaps the best photographic record of the day, to which, from time to time, he would refer—particularly to the shot he had taken as Steele and Green lambasted Ned Belknaps' bottom with their belts, when Newman had crawled beneath the struggling teacher and snapped the shutter, thus capturing not merely those red and dancing buttocks, but Ned's half-hard dick, his juggling balls, and his asshole, the ribbon at the end of that commemorative baseball trophy flying from it like a flag. That photo, for some reason, never failed to give Newman a roaring hardon when he looked on it, which he did whenever he had some rare private time at the Academy, and ever more frequently after he moved on to the State University on a wrestling scholarship.

In college, Newman truly came into his own as an athlete, in part due to his attitude and dedication, in part due to his coach, the legendary Mr. Drum. Newman worshiped the ground the man walked on—a champion during his own college career, a Olympian, and a legendary trainer of young men truly committed to the mat. Small, compact, and muscular, approaching forty with his dark blond hair buzzcut, Drum took a shine to Newman as well. Here was a kid who really did give 110%. Who not only listened to his coach's counsel but actually followed his advice; who trained as hard as he had to. On top of that, Drum liked Newman's "nice Jewish boy" persona—polite, thoughtful, and anxious to please.

The day the bond between the older and younger man began to change was just before the Regional Tournament. There was real concern that Newman would not make weight. He was a good half-pound over, and the meet was only hours away. He assured the coach he would avoid any liquids and spend whatever time it took in the sauna, but Drum would have none of it.

"The last thing we need is you dehydrated!" he barked. "There's a lot easier way to handle this."

Newman blushed deeply. He knew, of course, what Coach had in mind. He had often heard of this particular treatment being employed to help wrestlers lower their weight for the weigh-in. But he had never actually experienced... an enema; a long, deep, cleansing enema; an enema administered by his coach, Mr. Drum, whom he idolized.

"Skin outta your clothes and get back to the training room. I'll be there in a sec," Coach said.

Newman obediently did as he was told, noting the amused smiles of a couple of his team mates as he undressed and then headed back to where he'd been told.

Once there, he sat down on the cold metal table and waited. It wasn't that he was embarrassed about Coach seeing him naked or anything, for God's sake. But this was going to be so...intimate. And in that instant, the very instant Mr. Drum came through the doorway with a large, stainless steel canister sloshing intimidatingly held in his hand and a long length of white tubing slung over his shoulder, Newman flashed on that photo of Ned Belknaps red rear, spread, with that ribbon dangling out of his butthole.

"Okay, boy, get in the old fraternity position!" the coach said heartily.

Newman, a little confused, hopped off the table and then

bent forward over it.

"No, no, boy. Haven't you done this before? Up on the table. Nose down. Butt up. Spread your knees."

He said this with what, to Newman, seemed amazing nonchalance. But he obeyed, of course.

He cheek against the cold steel of the table, again—without his willing it—that image of his teacher returned to him, the one that always gave him such a bone. And here he was, presenting his furry little fanny to Coach, not for spanking, but still... Newman knew he was displaying pretty much anything a guy had to offer: his dick, his nuts, his rear, his crack, and his tight little slimslit—that wouldn't be tight for long.

Helplessly, he felt his cock begin to stiffen.

"First, son, I'm gonna grease you up."

Newman trembled as he felt the older man's finger—cool with a gob of KY—move gently around his rump ring, massaging it slightly, and then softly probing his sphincter, each poke entering deeper and deeper.

"At first, you'll feel like you need to piss and shit all at the same time," Mr. Drum said matter-of-factly, "but that'll pass."

Pop! Coach's digit slipped into Newman's rectum. Suddenly, his dick, which had been about half-hard, upshifted to full attention. The young man moaned.

"Okay." Mr. Drum seemed oblivious to Newman's boner. "Now, we just slide in this nozzle."

Newman glanced back. Oh, Jesus! That was a big sucker! It was vaguely bomb-shaped, with a whole series of holes in it.

"Now, son. This was hurt a little bit at first, but you just gotta stand it."

Groan! Newman felt that immensity resting again his greased pucker, and the tip of it begin its invasion. It was huge! Newman, in all his time at the Academy, had managed to retain his buttcherry, and now he was losing it not to dick, but to the cold metal nozzle of an enema tube!

And it was Coach who was taking his cherry. Newman

took a deep breath. Oh, God! The image of Ned Belknaps flitted again across his consciousness. Here he was with his ass stuck in the air, spread wide, so wide that Mr. Drum could probably count the hairs around his butthole! And Mr. Drum was pushing this... thing up inside him, and—Oh, God!, it was so humiliating and yet... he wanted to please Coach so bad.

"AHHHH!" he yowled as the monster-nozzle was suddenly devoured by his anus, as if it had always been hungry for something big and hard.

Coach rested his hand lightly on Newman's back. "Just get used to it, boy. It'll take a minute. Then we'll douche you out."

That warmth there just at the top of his crack. The massiveness there inside him. Newman's cock drooled a little precum. Oh, no! What would Mr. Drum think! But he couldn't help it. He could feel his rectal walls exploring the nozzle inside him—tentatively at first. Then it felt almost as if they molded themselves around it.

Coach drew away. "I think you're ready, boy. Now, this is gonna be uncomfortable at first, but you can stand it. I want you to take this whole bucket up in there and, when we get all the shit out of you, you'll be good to go." Newman heard a sharp click. "Now, if you start to cramp, tell me right off."

Suddenly, deep inside, Newman felt a warm oozing, which started to expand and grow and grow some more. His guts were being flooded.

"Take deep breaths!" Coach barked.

Newman gasped again and again. He felt a little light-headed. Coach's hand was on the small of his back again.

"That's a boy. We're about halfway home."

Halfway! Newman closed his eyes. But when he did, it was that picture of his teacher's ass that rose up, followed by, superimposed with, his imagined image of what he looked like in that very instant. He was under Mr. Drum's control as completely in that moment as the bound Ned Belknaps had been there tied to that steampipe. And his dick was hard as a pike. And he knew then—he really liked being under a man—this man's--control right now.

He felt a sudden stab in his gut. "Ow! Oh, I'm cramping."

"Just relax." The coach's voice was soothing, guttural. "It's okay. Relax." And to his mixed horror and pleasure, Newman felt Coach's hand on his belly, just below his belly, wedged between his gut and his screamingly hard dick, softly rubbing, trying to help him get past the tightness. Oh, God! Coach could feel the immense boner he was sporting! What would be think!

"Breathe deep. It'll pass," Mr. Drum cooed gruffly.

Suddenly, his other hand slipped from Newman's waist down his buns, right to the place where the nub of the nuzzled peeked out his asshole.

"Clench your cheeks." It was almost a whisper.

In a haze of humiliation, discomfort, and lust, Newman did as he was told.

The coach then squeezed those clamped buns even more tightly shut. "Keep breathin' deep. We're almost done."

The younger man drew in air. Expelled it. The pain in his gut slowly passed. He was adrift. Dreamy. He could feel the water pushing deeper and deeper inside him.

"Good, boy!" Mr. Drum suddenly said. "Now. Just hold all that for a couple of minutes.

Newman didn't think he could. The pressure inside him seemed unbearable. But he then let himself fall into the weird pleasure the whole experience was giving him—the feel of the man's rough hands on his rear, his tummy, those gentle strokes brushing now and again his cummy pole. He could have that go on forever.

"Okay, Newman. Now's the hard part!" the Coach chuckled. "I'm gonna pulled the plug on you, so get your hand back here. I want you to shove a couple fingers up your butthole and make a run for the shitter. Just clench hard."

Newman giggled. This all seemed so crazy.

"Here we go!"

"AHHH!"

The nozzle plowed out of his pucker, and he could feel water beginning to seep after it, threatening to flood. He reached back and jammed three fingers up his ass, rolled off the table, and hightailed it, as best he could, for the can.

"You can make it, boy!" The coach called after him.

He did. Barely. He was already leaking badly by the time he hit the porcelain rim, and the instant his cheeks spread, liquid gushed out of him in a geyser.

As his one hand was blown away from his butthole by the force of the spew, his other reached frantically for his dick, which felt as if it might explode as violently as his guts. Its explosion was not quite so extreme, but nonetheless cum arched high in the air and spattered on the half-closed stall door, and then continued to spurt and finally bubble from his piss slit as his bowels continued to clench and grasp, expelling what seemed a limitless stream into the bowl.

Newman crumpled forward, utterly exhausted. He heard a voice.

"You okay, boy?"

"Yes, sir! Yes, Coach!" he sputtered. God, he was a mess, and there was his juice dripping all over the place!

"Okay, when you're back together, come out and we'll check that weight. Here!" The coach heaved a couple of wet towels over the stall wall. "Clean yourself up good and then you can suit up."

Newman made weight, and took second in his class in the tournament. Not bad for a freshman bumped up to the varsity.

But he had wanted first.

He was mortified by his performance when he got that enema. There's no way the coach could have ignored his huge hard-on, and he had to wonder if the older man knew he had jerked off the minute he hit the can. What a perve he was! Oh, God!

And yet, Newman couldn't get that moment out of his

head. How he must've looked; that nozzle entering him; the sensation of that flood up his guts; the warmth of Coach's hands on his back, his buns, his gut, brushing his boner. Just thinking of it made him hard, and much as he despised himself for it, he wanted to feel all those sensations again. He wanted Mr. Drum to touch him.

And mixed with this were the images of Mr. Belknaps' punishment. All alone, Newman would review those photographs again and again, feeling a huge excitement, imagining it was him, not his teacher, who was subject to such spanking, such humiliation. He thought somehow his experience with the tube and Ned Belknaps' with the cane and paddle and hairbrush and belt must be somehow alike.

An idea came to him. He was determined to act.

"Coach, I'm just not satisfied with my performance."

It was after practice, and Newman had lingered so as to speak to Mr. Drum privately.

"Hey, you're a freshman, Newman. You've got..."

"I'm not giving my all, though, Coach. I know I can do better. I just need some, ah, motivation."

"I think your motivations pretty good, son. You..."

"I can do better, Sir," Newman interrupted. He felt daring, scared. "Back at the Academy, when we didn't perform up to snuff, Coach Mann would paddle us."

He tried so hard to make it sound unremarkable, and yet he knew that one word, "paddle," hung there in the air.

Mr. Drum looked at him curiously. "You think you need to be paddled to do your best?"

"Yes, Sir. I dunno. I mean..." Newman realized he was losing it. He took a deep breath and tossed his head. "I don't know, Sir! It just always worked with me."

The coach shrugged. "Well, you were a kid then. I don't think that..."

"I really think it would help, Coach," Newman pleaded. "I mean, I know it sounds kinda weird, but I wouldn't even mention it except that I've just been disappointed in myself. I figured I could tell you." He lowered his eyes.

The silence seemed so long. Then, Mr. Drum snorted a laugh. "Well, hell, Newman. If you figure a swat on the butt'll get you wired, I'll give you a couple."

"Thanks, Sir. I'll come early tomorrow. You'll see!"

And with that, Newman fled the office, filled with triumph. And terror! What had he done? What had he gotten himself into? Mr. Drum into? And yet...

Next day, he arrived early. It was dinnertime. The locker room was deserted.

"Coach?"

"Back here, Newman."

Mr. Drum was in the training room. Newman closed the door behind him.

"Well, turn around, boy. What'll it be? Three?"

"No, Sir. Six at least." Newman reach in his gym bag and pulled out a frat paddle he had bought at the bookstore. "Here."

A look, both perplexed and almost suspicious, passed across the coach's face. He paused. "You're serious about this, aren't you, Newman."

"Yes, Sir. I am." Newman turned around and unbuckled his pants.

"You want these bareass!" Mr. Drum asked incredulously.

"Oh, yes, sir. That's how we always got'em at the Academy."

Newman bent forward on the table.

A long instant passed. Then...

WHACK!

The paddle landed squarely across both of Newman's cheeks. He yiked loudly. He had forgotten just how bad a paddle could burn! But he steadied himself. "Yes, Sir. Thank you, Sir. May I have another, Sir!"

WHACK!

Newman took six. His butt was in flames. The coach, once committed to the mission, had not held back at all, but wielded the paddle with devastating force. The younger man rubbed his buns furiously, still facing away from Mr. Drum so as not to show his blooming erection.

The paddle clattered to the floor.

"Okay, son. I did it for you. I better see some results tomorrow."

And results he did see. Newman knew he would have to demonstrate how this particular motivator pushed him beyond limits he might normally be expected to traverse. The next day, and the day after, he was a tiger on the mat, and Mr. Drum was impressed.

"Maybe we could dose me up again," Newman suggested.

"Whatever you say, mister. As long as I keep seeing this kind of improvement."

And so Newman arranged to have his naked fanny paddled at least twice weekly by the coach he adored. Baring himself, humbling himself, displayed himself before Coach; asking for him to blister his rear—this intoxicated Newman. After a spanking, he would dash back to the dorm and look at his rump in the mirror, glorying in its redness and heat. He would rub and soothe it, imaging his were Coach's hands, and then take to drubbing his dick while still stroking and fingering himself till he blew wad after wad of juice.

Insodoing, he allowed himself to imagine other things—feeling Coach's hands all over him, trying to guess what the man's dick was like, how his asshole smelled. He would dream of Mr. Drum one day simply overpowering him and having his way with him.

In the paddling, Newman kept upping the ante. "Let's do eight, Sir... ten... twelve..."

WHACK! WHACK! WHACK!

On the day he requested fourteen swats, his life—and that of Coach Drum—changed forever.

That evening, for some reason, he was nervous. He couldn't figure it. He wasn't scared of a couple extra swats. His tushie had become tougher and tougher as the spankings had continued. But somehow, it was as if this couldn't go on forever, and that even this game he was playing was insufficient to his real needs.

WHACK!

As the eleventh stroke landed, Newman's dick shivered. He had a full erection, something that has usually passed from the pain by this time.

WHACK!

On the twelfth, he began to shudder all over.

WHACK!

On the thirteenth, helplessly, his cock spasmed and a glob of sperm jetted from his slit.

WHACK!

Fourteen! His balls suddenly squeezed and cum was flying everywhere! His ravaged bottom was clenching and unclenching. He danced from foot to foot. A puddle of spooge gathered on the floor.

Newman began to cry.

He just stood there, his dick still dripping, his rump in flames, tears streaming from his eyes. He hands went to his face. Shit! He was so sick. He was such a faggot! Coach would see now he was just a fucking...

"Settle down, boy," a voice growled.

And then, he felt a pair of strong arms embrace him, pulling him tight.

"It's okay, Newman. It's okay."

The young man abandoned himself to long, deep sobs. "Sir. I'm sorry. I'm so sorry. I didn't mean to..."

"Don't fret, Newman. Get it out."

The wrestler grabbed his coach and bawled like some six year old, and his coach held him, there with his pants down, till the boy had begun to settle.

Then, Newman heard a throaty whisper. "Get it out, boy.

I know what you want."

Gently, Mr. Drum pushed Newman onto his knees. The young man faced the crotch of the older man's gym shorts. He caught an intoxicating whiff of the musk emanating from where he could see an immense bulge.

"Get it out, boy. It's okay."

Newman pulled back the leg of Mr. Drum's gym shorts, then his jockstrap. A veiny, seven inch dick, hard as stone, thrust out. Though Newman had never in his life sucked dick, his mouth immediately enveloped the lustrous, satiny head of that manpole, and he deliciously slurped it as deep as he could.

It took only minutes for spurt after spurt of shimmering juice to fill his mouth, dribble down his gullet, leak from his lips and drool down his chin. The young man collapsed on the floor, spattered with both the coach's cum and his own.

Coach Drum squatted beside him.

"Newman," he said softly, "if you want, we can forget this ever happened. Or you can show up here tomorrow at noon, and we'll take a ride over to my place, and we'll have a little talk, and maybe I can show you some holds you never dreamed of."

And then he stood, and walked out.

The rest, as you might expect, is history. Filled with embarrassment and shame, Newman nonetheless did go to the gym next day at noon, and endured an uncomfortable ride with the coach to his small house. Once there, over coffee, Mr. Drum informed him that, from early on, he had been on to Newman's game. The young man's excitement during his enema was something seen hundreds of times before, and the paddling proposal—though unique—was still oblique enough that Drum could not be sure of his young athlete's intentions. But he had not missed Newman's roaring erections when he was getting spanked, and, not only that, but found he himself hardening as the prospect of each new smacking of those furry but boyish cheeks. Still, of course, given his position, he could make no sign. Frankly, the paddlings—even if voluntarily submitted to—were enough to get him fired.

But he had long ago realized that he was simply not particularly interested in women, and had, when on the road, had
a few experiences with men, which, though pleasant enough,
had never really meant more than a nice opportunity to get off.
When this fine, youthful specimen had wandered into his office
that day and proposed he be paddled, he wondered if, finally, he
had found a male he could truly let into his world.

Newman, literally, wept for joy, and it was only minutes
before he was on his knees again, nuzzling the coach's crotch.
Mr. Drum allowed this for a few minutes, before he stood and
took the wrestler by the hand and led him to the bedroom.

Newman began to rip his clothes off, but before he could
get very far, the hard voice of Coach stopped him.

"Boy! You're gonna get all the dick you want and more
this afternoon. But before that, sonny, you've got a real spanking
coming!"

And with that, he took Newman by the ear, led him over to
the bed, sat down, pulled down the boy's pants, and hauled him
over his knee. He then proceeded to literally blister that tight,
athletic fanny—first with his hand, and then, reaching over to the
night table, with a wooden hairbrush. Newman danced frantically
around, kicked his legs in the air, but Coach was unrelenting, and
it was only when the younger man was crying and begging that
the spanking finally stopped.

That first time, they didn't even have their clothes off. Mr.
Drum flipped Newman onto the mattress and pulled his rear end
up in the air. He plunged his face into that hairy crack and begin
to rim that sweaty manring furiously.

"Oh, God! Oh, God, yes!" Newman blubbered, the last
of his tears mixing with the ecstasy of a tongue probing his most
secret spot.

"Fuck, boy! You are so tight! Jesus, you smell so hot!"
Coach moaned.

It was only minutes later that Newman heard a fly unzipped,
spit hawked, and then—for real—surrendered his buttcherry. At

first it was painful, and the rub of slacks again his sore behind hurt, but with only a little time he was pleading for even deeper penetration, for longer strokes, for simple, harder fucking!

That whole afternoon they gave over to sex. Like proverbial kids in a candy store, they explored each other utterly, and Drum himself offered up his own hole to Newman for deflowering.

At five, the Coach dressed hurriedly and headed for practice.

At the door of the bedroom, he turned. "I'll put you on the roster as sick," he smiled. "If this is all you wanted, get your shit together and be out of here before seven-thirty. No mention will ever be made of what's happened. You're not off the team or anything. But if you're not serious, then go." He paused. "If you are serious, then stay right here, and we'll have at it some more." He winked. "Just in case, I'm picking up a paddle at the bookstore on my way home."

It was, as the old saying goes, the beginning of a beautiful friendship. One that continues to this day.

THE COMMANDANT:

As it happens, all these particular turns of events—though Newman or Selwen or Steele and Green would have never dreamt it--would not have entirely surprised the other protagonist of our story: The Commandant, Mr. Knighten.

The very evening of the "Incident at Brownsfield Academy," Knighten returned to his neat bungalow, where he lived alone. As soon as he was through the door, he placed a phone call. There was no answer at the other end, merely the electronic voice of the answering machine.

"Request permission to speak with you, Sir!" was all The Commandant said.

He removed his resplendent tunic, and, in his uniform pants and a t-shirt, microwaved his dinner. He ate standing up, and then, at 7:30 p.m. precisely, descended the stairs to the basement. There, he reached behind the washing machine and removed a key, with which he unlocked a padlock on a door in the wall which divided the cellar roughly in half.

Inside was room with walls entirely covered in mirrors with a dusty cement floor. It's only furnishings were a table upon which sat a speaker phone and, in the corner, a manikin dressed in a bird colonel's uniform, with a pair of splendidly shined boots spread before them.

Before entering the room, the Commandant stripped in the doorway, reverently, to nothing but his socks, draping his clothes neatly on a nearby hanger. As he removed each item of dress, nothing seemed amiss until the burly man lowered his underwear. Observing him from the front, what anyone would note is that, just below the waistline, the abundant hair that pelted his chest and hard and protuberant belly suddenly and unexpectedly ceased. His gut, crotch, and balls were absolutely smooth, as devoid of hair as the nether regions of the merest boy.

Just below his waist was a tight, quite narrow belt of leather, from which extended two straps that framed his hairless crotch and disappeared between his legs. Meanwhile, around the neck of his penis, just below the head, was a black leather collar. It was attached to two bands which were themselves connected to a strap that circled Mr. Knighten's balls tightly. As a consequence of this arrangement, it was immediately apparent that The Commandant was completely prevented from achieving a full erection. The short, tight bands restricted his cock's ability to extend itself, so, even in the most intense excitement, he would be unable to get a full hardon.

Around in back, the observer would be in store for another, though similar surprise. The fur that appeared even on his lower back vanished at the swell of his buttocks, which were hairless as any nine year old's, even to the very depths of his crack. Across his rear were the faint, pink shadows of parallel lines. Meanwhile, at his anus was a two inch circle of rubber, the outer end of a fist-shaped buttplug buried deep in Knighten's own rectum. Not merely was this particular "anal intruder" designed to imitate the size of the small adult male hand, but decorated in an almost medieval way on its plastic surface with numerous grommets and spikes, so that these might poke and probe in unexpected ways the walls of the rectum.

When he was nude but for his socks, Knighten sat and laced his boots on again, then went into the room and closed the door.

There, he stood at strict attention before the phone, never moving, though as time passed, sweat began to drip from his bearish armpits. His rump would clench now and again, and his cock would strain against its bonds.

At 8:05, the phone rang.

The Commandant darted forward and punched the "speak" button, then snapped immediately back to attention.

"What the hell do you want, scumbag!" a voice growled from the phone.

"Request permission to describe the day's events, SIR!"

Knighten answered.

There was an extended pause. Then the voice on the other end of the line said wearily, "All right, Knighten! But be quick about it!"

"Yes, Sir!" The Commandant barked.

He then began his narration of the punishment of Ned Belknaps. He described in detail encountering Ned masturbating in the men's room, his infuriated response, his dragging the teacher with his pants down out of the restroom and into the hall. He lovingly recalled the three sharp smacks on the instructor's bare bottom in the hallway, and exposing him in his humiliated state to the cadets of his class. Then, precisely and with great gusto, he described the various spankings to which the masturbating Mr. Belknaps' had been subject—the slashing thrashing with the pointer, the pounding paddling by the cadets themselves, and the sizzling spanking with the hairbrush that had finally driven the thirty-five year old over the edge into the realm of a wailing little boys. He then recounted spreading that brightly burnished behind across his knee and smacking the miscreant directly on his quivering anus, violating that hole with his finger as he did so. He recalled how he had forced Ned's penis to get hard and displayed him thus before the sniggering cadets, then had stuffed his shorts in his mouth and spanked him down the corridor before the assembled entirety of the school.

He then told the anonymous man at the other end of the line how he had had the misbehaving and thoroughly blistered instructor tied to the steam pipe and displayed, how he had used the dunce cap to humiliate him further, and ravished his asshole with that old baseball trophy. He described the excitement of Steele and Green as they had been given permission to lay their straps across Belknaps' blazing and incapacitated ass, and that of the other cadets there with their cameras. He detailed almost verbatim his threat as to Belknaps' punishment in upcoming days for any tardiness or insubordination.

Throughout all this, Mr. Knighten tried to keep his voice steady, but it was difficult. It would rise and fall, thin now and then, revealing his intense excitement. Not merely that, he was prone, though he tried to remain at attention, to sudden shudders and shakes. His buttcheeks would grasp suddenly, then release as rapidly as that plug deep in his anus poked his rectal walls, his substantial buttocks wiggling uncontrollably. His cock, meanwhile, strained against its bonds, again and again reaching for erection, trying to rise from his hairless crotch, only to be restrained by those short and unforgiving leather straps.

By the time he was done speaking, the Commandant was panting, his lust virtually limitless.

For a moment, there was only the sound of his labored breathing.

Then, from the phone, the voice rasped. "Very good, Knighten. Sounds like a good session of humiliation, punishment, spanking, domination, and discipline! One neither this Belknaps nor your boys will soon forget." There was a pause. "So, scumbag, what do you want ME to do about it!"

"Sir," the Commandant said weakly. "Sir, please, request permission to...to..."

There was a sharp laugh from the speaker. "To WHAT, Knighten! Speak up, you friggin' pussy!"

"Re-request permission to... to... to COME, SIR!"

There was momentary silence, then more laughter, harsh and brutal. "Come! You want to COME, you miserable dickbreath? Hah!" The voice fell to a low, menacing tone. "You think you have EARNED coming, you little shit?"

"Yes, Sir! Pl...pl...please, Sir!" Knighten whined.

There was another long period of quiet. "When are you next scheduled to report, Knighten."

"A week from Sunday, Sir."

"That's awfully close, scumbag. If you disappointment me, it will cost you. You know that!"

"Yes, Sir! Yes, Sir! Please, I won't disappoint you!"

"This is going to cost you anyway, you cumwad! Just the request will cost you!" the voice snarled. Then there was a hiss. "All right, Knighten. Release that miserable little pecker of yours!"

With an audible sigh, the Commandant reached down and unscrewed the tiny bolts that held the straps to the collar around his penis. His dick almost instantly shot out from his crotch to a full 7, thick inches, and a drop of manhoney appeared on its tip.

"Stand at attention, turdball! Don't you even THINK of touching that prick of yours!"

"No, Sir! NEVER! NO, SIR!" Knighten roared, quivering all over, but braced smartly before the phone.

"All right, pig!" the voice shouted. "Position yourself!"

"Yes, Sir!"

The Commandant hurried to the far corner of the room, where he immediately threw himself face down on the floor with a loud SLAP.

After a moment, the voice snarled, "Very well, WORM! Approach the BOOTS!"

Knighten emitted something between a groan and a sigh of relief. Then, very slowly, he began to squirm across the floor, his tongue extended from his mouth, licking the cold and dirty cement as he slowly and deliberately advanced. His dripping, turgid cock scraped painfully on the concrete as, inch by inch, he moved forward. Snaking his way over the ground, the forty-five year old Marine's broad, meaty, hairless buttocks with their ghostly pink stripes would rise and fall in the air, revealing the nub of the massive buttplug planted deep in his rectum. With each small advance, the grommets and spines of that plug would scrape and poke at the tender manspace deep within him. He whinnied and whined with each movement, but still the Commandant continued on his belly toward his goal, his lolling tongue and weeping penis creating thin, damp lines across the filthy floor.

"Be quick about it, WORM!" the voice demanded. "I don't have all goddamn night!"

It took a full five minutes, but finally the Commandant knelt before the uniformed manikin of the colonel. His mouth was dry and dusty, his cock tender and slightly skinned, but his eyes were alight, fixed on those beautiful boots!

"Sir! Mission accomplished, Sir!"

The voice over the speakerphone sighed. "Very well, dirt-bag! Take your reward. BUT NO HANDS!"

"No, Sir! No, Sir!" Knighten yelped joyously, then plunged his face deep into one of the empty boots, sniffing the stiff scent of a sweaty, masculine foot. The old, slightly rancid smell seemed to work on him like a drug. He began to chew and lick the hard, shiny leather, whimpering and snorting. With his hands clasped tightly behind his back, as if at parade rest, he plunged his face into the boots, his rump grasping and squirming as the buttplug squirreled madly about up his shaved anus, scraping and prob-ing. He ultimately planted one of his own feet beneath him as he lapped at and worried the boots like a big dog, bouncing his butt up and down on the hard heel of his own gleaming shoe so as to plough the plug ever more profoundly into his anxious and agonized asshole!

The process did not take long. The Commandant began to quiver all over, shaking and shuddering, and raised his head suddenly into the air. He let out a howl like a wolf baying at the moon. The pitch rose steadily up the scale, into a shriek, as the muscles of his massive rump contracted violently, and a gob of semen shot from the slit of his dick. The wad was immense, but nonetheless followed by another of even greater size, then another! His penis, his balls, his rear, his entire body spasmed helplessly as juice poured from his cock in a steady stream, almost as if he were pissing, as if a dam had broken, and an entire reservoir of mancome stored within him rushed for release. He babbled incomprehensibly, completely at the mercy of his wildly blasting manroot as his orgasm went on and on! All the excitement and desire of the last two weeks, of blister-ing Sergeant Pierce's furry tail across his knee, of punishing the naked backsides of Slopes and Paine, of smacking the exposed behinds of cadet after cadet, and most of all the thrill of publicly spanking and humiliating the masturbating Ned Belknaps in front of the entire company of cadets of Brownsfield Academy, roared from deep within him and spattered the walls and the floor of his basement.

During this spectacle, the voice on the phone was silent. Only after the Commandant emitted a deep groan of satisfaction and lay panting on the cold cement did it echo once again through that silent space.

"You're a fucking pig, Knighten! Clean up after yourself. NOW!"

"Yes, Sir! YES, SIR!" The Commandant puffed.

He immediately began to lick up the mess he had made, pushing his face into his own cum, smearing it on his nose, his cheeks, and his chin. He cooed and gurgled like a baby as he sucked up his own sticky, sparkling juice, even though now, his orgasm done, the pain and fullness up his asshole was almost unbearable for the mighty plug shoved up him.

Again, there was a period of silence.

When the voice came over the line again, it was low and threatening. "You will report as usual, Knighten."

"Yes, Sir!" The Commandant agreed breathlessly.

"For this, Knighten, you will receive an EXTRA thrashing. Do you understand!"

"Yes, Sir."

"I want a dozen of those willow switches, at least!"

"Oh, yes, Sir! Yes, SIR!"

"Oh, and Knighten, we will have company."

Knighten gulped and knit his brow. He knew he would not enjoy today's privilege without humiliating cost.

"A new recruit," the voice purred. "Just 19. His barracks buddies call him 'Long Dong.'" The voice chuckled. "I have told him only that he should report to me on Sunday morning, unshowered, in his combat boots. Caked with mud. You will be expected to treat him as your superior!"

"Yes, Sir!"

"He's a fine specimen, Knighten. He will enjoy watching me thrash you silly, I am sure."

"Yes, Sir!"

"Perhaps I'll have him thrash you, too, scumbag," the voice added, "precisely for this lack of control of yours!"

"Yes, Sir."

"Oh, and Knighten, remember his nickname. It's a full 11 inches, so I have heard. You'll be handcuffed, of course, so you can imagine how you will be servicing it! He's half-Arab, so they say, which means he's hairy as a bear as well."

"Yes, Sir!"

"Enough, dogshit!" the voice suddenly barked. "I will see you on Sunday!"

And then the phone cut off.

The Commandant lay naked on the floor. Though exhausted, he could imagine what awaited him the following week. He could taste the dried mud of a private's boots in his mouth, the unwashed funk of a 19 year old's well-furred asshole on his tongue. At least, he thought, as an Arab, he was probably circumcised. How he hated the flavor of smegma deep in his gullet!

There would be his commander's boots to be spitshined as well, of course, and it was difficult to imagine just how totally his buttocks would be switched, again and again, with the willow, just as his father had used on him so long ago. His poor rear would be in flames, and that fire would not stop, but only rage brighter and hotter! His hands cuffed behind his back, there would be no way to save his ass from the burning kiss of those ravishing rumproasters!

And then, of course, there would be the humiliation of kneeling before his superior officer, as a young private prepared to plow his quivering anus. How his commander seemed to enjoy subjecting him to the indignity of merciless buttfucking by the youngest and most amply endowed recruits to the Corps! A "long dong" of 11 inches! It would feel like it was coming out his mouth! And surely a length of that size would be matched with a massive girth as well! Thank God he was forced to wear a buttplug to prepare his rectum for an invasion of such magnitude.

Naked on the floor, though, he could imagine how he would come. His dick would spew again and again. He would enjoy orgasm after orgasm, throughout and despite—or was it because of?—the thrashings, the blowjobs, the ass-eating, the bootlicking, the buttfucking. He would expel load after manly load from his frothing balls, without ever so much as TOUCHING his own dick!

Such was Commandant Knighten, then—himself a man utterly in thrall to the kind of authority he himself exercised. The very day of his whipping for playing with himself, he had discovered something amazing. Left alone with his pants still down, he had tried to rub the terrible sting from his welted bottom. To his astonishment, his pecker, which when standing before his father had been but a tiny nub, grew and grew, soon standing out before him like a jutting flagpole. As he massaged his rear further, a tingle arose in his nuts, and, before he knew it, his rear end was grasping madly as he blew shot after shot of teenage come from his erect prick!

Terrified his orgasm might be discovered, he dropped to his knees and, employing the only cleaning implement available, tongued up the puddle of gyzm from the cold, concrete floor of the basement.

Still, he was amazed! He had encountered the way to ejaculate without laying a finger on his own member!

From that point on, his terror of his father's switch was, at least, somewhat alleviated by the promise of the solitary pleasure that would come after. After his enlistment in the Corps at eighteen, his horizons had widened considerably. He had, of course, learned to plough pussy with the best of them. However, early on in his military career, a superior officer had used him utterly—whipping his rump, pounding his throat, slamming dick up his asshole. Thus, Knighten had discovered further means by which he could avoid the temptation of masturbation ever after.

Five years before, he had met a retired Colonel who lived only two hours away, only too willing to take him on as his personal scumboy. After that, women held no allure. He had found his place in life. Each spanking he administered—to bare cadet rump, to Pierce's squirming fanny, to Paine and Slopes's rears, even to Ned Belknaps' bare bottom—was merely a way for him to store up yet more of his precious manjuice, to be expelled from his spasming dick while naked and roaring beneath the hard eyes of his superior.

Knighten rose slowly, painfully from the cement. With resignation, he connected once again the straps that restrained his penis. There must be no accidents in bed tonight!

And then, naked but for his boots, the Commandant strode manfully from his secret room in the basement, imagining tomorrow what discipline he would have to impose upon whatever naked male buttocks presented themselves for punishment.

How grand it was that SPANKING had been invented!

It was good to be alive!

ABOUT THE AUTHOR

eddie knapps was born in Oklahoma and has lived in various places in both the United States and abroad. Over the years, he has published both fiction and non-fiction, as well as erotica in such magazines as Manscape, FirstHand, Red Tails, and other. This is his first book-length fetish publication.

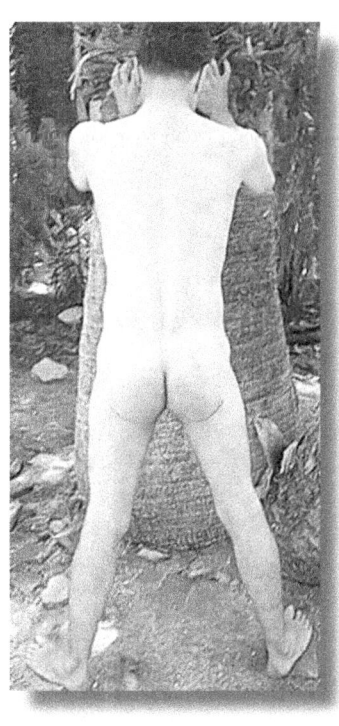

www.ingramcontent.com/pod-product-compliance
Lightning Source LLC
Chambersburg PA
CBHW071226260626
47162CB00004B/1443